The Drummer Boy: Grey and

By

C.G. Buswell

Also by C.G. Buswell

Novels

Grey and Scarlet 1: The Grey Lady Ghost of the Cambridge Military Hospital

Short Stories

Christmas at Erskine

Halloween Treat

Though this is a work of fiction, there are historical events, names, places and characters portrayed throughout the novel. These are imagined by the author to allow the drummer boy's tale to be told as he imagines it.

For my beloved son, Angus, the brightest star in heaven. My angel, forever in my heart.

Chapter 1

He flinched as the cat o' nine tails dug deep into his back, blood spurting out as its eighteen inches of tightened rope whipped back with a crack. The nine twisted cords with their wire-bound ends that were designed to inflict extreme pain were once more lashed viciously towards him with a violent sound like sudden crackling lightning. They reached through his scarred back, delving through his skin, penetrating layers of muscle and fat to reach the sensitive nerves where they could cause more pain.

He would not cry out, he had promised himself, he must make them proud; he must beat his drum for the rhythm of the other, much older drummer boys to continue the punishment of the man who was stripped bare before them. The prisoner wore no kilt because he did not want his blood, sweat, faeces and urine that he knew he would void to stain his garment. The prisoner still had to serve in General Wellington's army despite his desertion at the Battle of Arroyo dos Molinos on 28 October 1811. He was new to the Gordon Highlanders, the 92nd Regiment of Foot, and was scared. He knew this punishment was not just an example to the thousands of men standing on parade in the cold rain of a foreign land, but that it was also designed to break him and toughen him up for the battles that were to come in this brutal Peninsular War. He shivered not just from fear, but as an automatic nervous response to the pain and cold, yet the whipping warmed him to the core, with anger, rage and humiliation. He vowed *he would take his punishment like a man, 1000 lashes for desertion. His sergeant had told him to expect 100 in each parade. He would be taken back in front of the others, maybe a week later, once his flesh had healed and he could walk again. More indignation and more lashes would open up his welt scarred back. Nine more punishment parades: if he lived. He was reassured that most officers would halt the punishment flogging at each 100, though he had known some prisoners to survive 500 before the senior officer signalled for the lashings to stop. He had lost count but knew that in the past no-one had ever survived 1000 lashes at one time, before a Royal Commission in 1838 had reduced the number of maximum lashes at one time to two-hundred. He would not benefit from the abolition of this barbaric punishment by the army many years later in 1881.*

His bladder had involuntary voided as he was tied to the Battalion sergeant's halberts, momentarily warming his legs and staining the earth under him. These three long lances were secured to the ground and tied in a triangle to which he had been secured with rope which dug deep into his wrists. His ankles were bound to the bottom of each lance, forcing him into the indignity of being spread-eagled. As the lashing started his bowels voided and his waste involuntary fell into a steaming pile between his heels. The junior officer beside him turned his nose away in contempt at the act and the smell. He reached into his tunic pocket and withdrew a silk handkerchief. He held this against his delicate nose to show his disgust and in a vain effort to conceal the smell. This

6

added to the prisoner's humiliation in front of people who should have been his

friends and comrades. With whom he should have fought and killed French

soldiers in the frenzy of battle. Instead he had run in the opposite direction but

was soon captured by the Provosts, here to police the Allied armies of the

British, Portuguese and Spanish troops. His crime of deserting in the face of the

enemy was seen as too severe to run the gauntlet where a prisoner must walk

along his fellow ranks and be struck a blow by every member of the regiment

with a stick or raw hide.

Instead the drummer boys were told not to spare their lashes on fear of their

own punishment. They each took turns to lash out with all the might two

fourteen year olds could muster to bring the 15-inch handle with its evil

payload upon the bleeding flesh of this grown man before them. His flayed back

was looking more like a street map of raised twists and turns that within

minutes would resemble more of a slab of meat on a butcher's block where

muscle and fat could be seen with no flesh evident but with blood aplenty. White

bones could be briefly glimpsed before each new cavity filled with fresh pouring

blood that ran down his body, soaking from his toes and into the foreign earth

forming a dark red mud bath beneath him. Their instructions of beating the sin

from the prisoner's flesh while instilling respect was upper-most in their minds

as they swung the cat o' nine tails for all they were worth, their juvenile sweat

reaching out to the younger boy whose face was already marked with the flayed

blood of the prisoner. All three were wishing secretly that they had joined a

7

cavalry or artillery regiment because their farriers performed this barbaric duty. Then they would not have felt guilty upon hearing the begging screams for mercy from the prisoner and his pitiful cries for his mother that poured forth from his loosened jaw which hung down and over-ran with snot from his nose and intermingled with his saliva. Even the most hardened of criminals within the army, the King's hard bargains as they were nicknamed, would always cry out for their mother or God for mercy. None deserved any and none was given. It would be many years before the rewards and praise system favoured by General Sir John Moore, the "Father of the British Infantry", would be introduced into this brutal British army. Many more would fall victim to this Drumhead Court-Martial system of punishment.

The ranks of soldiers were smartly turned out, rigid to attention with their muskets raised. Each wore their full dress of shoes, red and white hose, green shaded kilts: this new issue known as the Feilidh beag: the little kilt, because it now reached to just above the knee. Their much loved Regimental kilt with the yellow over-stripe was worn with their heavy red jackets with ornamental yellow cuffs and cross belts with ammunition pouches. Unlike the other infantry soldiers who wore the almost French-like shako small peaked caps, these mighty men proudly wore their bonnets with dyed black ostrich feathers between the cockade and the red, white and black felt chequered cloth. The dreich weather, reminiscent of their native Aberdeen, made the feathers floppy in this downpour. Their fellow Scotsmen of the Black Watch and the Cameron

Highlanders also wore these and all three regiments shared the same contempt for deserters. Only the officers wore a sporran, individually created to suit each personal preference, their Lieutenant favouring a tasselled badger fur sporran. Each, to a man, watched with scorn aimed towards the prisoner from their regimental hollow square surrounding the long spiked poles. No matter how long he served with the Gordon's, he would always be known as the one that fled in fear. Other regiments could forgive prisoners such as Corporal Pitt of the 95th Rifles who received 120 of his 300 sentenced lashes for trying to smuggle his wife aboard the ship at Ostend that took him to Spain, despite the orders of Colonel Sir Andrew Barnard. Though the Corporal was reduced to the ranks he still retained the respect of his men for taking his punishment well. But this snivelling, crying fool before them, who had soiled himself so quickly, would have to work very hard to gain any respect or trust, especially in battle. Each hardened warrior had been proud of their zero desertion rate against those of their fellow Scots regiments such as the 71st Highland Regiment of Light Infantry with three deserters this year alone. Most infantry or cavalry units had a desertion rate of ten a year. The Gordon's had been steadfast in their battles with General Wellington and had none. This cowardly man before them had dishonoured their proud regiment from the North East of Scotland and each man knew that the prisoner deserved every lash for breaking their trust and eagerly looked on for the next savage blow. They hoped that their Regimental Medical Officer, standing next to his medical chest, his pocket set of probes, forceps and scissors useless against such deep wounds, would not nod delicately to their Commanding Officer to signal that the man could take no more lashing. Those that could, eagerly counted with each painful stroke of the cat o' nine tails, the others fervently watched the efforts of the drummer boys to ensure they did their task to the best of their ability.

The drummer boy was too young to understand any of this or to have any empathy for the foul-smelling man before him. He just knew he had to do his duty, like his father had in the Walcheren Campaign in the Netherlands two years previously. To honour his father's sacrifice, he would beat rhythmically on his drum; no matter the pain, no matter that he had urinated into his kilt as the first lash struck the prisoner and caused the naked man before him to wail out like a trapped animal. 'Rubidub dum' went his drums time after time in response to the drumsticks in his tiny fingers. One stroke of the cat o' nine tails to every ten drum beats, he knew his hands, wrists and arms would ache, but he must continue to beat and beat his drum…

Chapter 2

Rubidub dum, rubidub dum went the drums, giving their order of battle above the cannons roaring, amongst the sound of swords clashing with steel and the tearing of flesh and the shattering of bone. Muskets gave off their popping sound as their white smoke filled the area, obscuring the vision of the soldiers, descending onto the battlefield like a morning mist settling on the dew. Though nowhere as peaceful; this was the most brutal of conflicts. Scott looked around him, taking in this scene of the Battle of Waterloo, Sunday 18th June 1815. He heard the roaring and war cry screams of men deep in battle, summoning up their courage from deep within, unleashing their inner demons, drawing up the strength to take another's life in animalistic fury. Their very survival was dependant on taking the lives of others. Scott could not smell the stench of battle he had expected: faeces, urine, rank body odour, blood and fear, but blood most of all. The indescribable coppery and salty reek that only a veteran could understand that cloyed in your nostrils and stayed for a few nauseous days in your nose, but a lifetime in the imagination. He did not miss it and was glad it was not present here to remind him of his own past wars, of Afghanistan and his heart-wrenching loss that only now, three years later he was coming to terms with, albeit slowly. It was a daily emotional battle, as bad to him as the physical battle of the invading French armies pitted against the might of the defending forces of the British, German, Dutch, Belgians and Prussians. It was the sudden

11

invasion three days ago of a well-armed Napoleon Bonaparte into Belgium against the Duke of Wellington and his Allies. This is what Scott had come to see and he was not altogether disappointed.

The battle played out as he thought it would and he was momentarily distracted as he thought back to his encounter with the Grey Lady ghost in his cherished, but now lonely flat back in Aldershot which was his sanctuary from army life. It had been built upon the site of the former Cambridge Military Hospital. The ghost of this former World War One nursing sister of the Queen Alexandra's Imperial Military Nursing Service, the QAIMNS, had foretold him that he had a gift, that he had to use it wisely and that he was able to go back to any battle, to meet army ghosts from the spirit world and help them to be laid to rest. He had felt burdened by this almighty task, but after his meeting with Jim at Erskine Nursing Home back in December he had been relishing his next encounter with a new restless phantom. Like the obedient soldier and nurse he was, he was ready to do this new duty, a duty that he could not reveal to anyone for fear of being ridiculed, or worse sectioned under the Mental Health Act!

Now he was watching his fellow Scot. The tall and commanding Sergeant Ewart of the proud Scots Greys, named after their magnificent and powerful grey horses. This cavalryman made his charge upon the French, and was about to take their Eagle, the much coveted standard that was said to bring the French luck because each had been touched by the hand of Napoleon. Scott could hear proud guttural shouts of 'Scotland Forever!' echo around him as others took up the rousing chant. With its capture came an instant order to leave the battlefield, and with it promotion, often to the rank of Lieutenant for other ranks soldiers who were usually too poor to buy a commission, like Sergeant Ewart had been. Most of all was the glory that waited at Headquarters as the recipient took his prize to the safety of the capital of Brussels, along with news of the battle. It was an accolade worth risking life and limb for, and many had made this sacrifice in a vain but brave attempt. Sergeant Ewart was sat upon his heavy charger. He was made all the taller with his bearskin worn on his sweating head, resplendent in his red tunic. He carved his way through the French soldiers, slashing furiously with his sabre against the drawn muskets of the enemy, constantly searching out their bodies through their uniform that parted easily with his highly honed blade as it sunk through meaty flesh as easily as carving a Sunday roast beef joint. The steel decimated vital organs and caused the enemy soldiers to fall like skittles. They were crushed beneath the galloping hooves of his trusted mount. Beside him was his junior officer, the young Ensign Francis Kinchant, though he was senior in rank, both of them knew, unsaid, that in the thick of the melee Sergeant Charles Ewart was the real commander. He was battle experienced and took it upon himself to be an unofficial field mentor to the inexperienced officer. In the height of battle, he rode on to where his comrades, James Armour, who was a relative of the poet Robert Burns' wife, Jean, and Dickson were nearing to the Eagle of the 45th Régiment de Ligne, the Regiment of the Line. Their gold lettered battle honours were fluttering in the light breeze flaunting its red, white and blue colours proudly on a coloured streamer below the golden coloured Eagle that in Scott's time would be on display in the Great Hall of Edinburgh Castle.

Scott was close enough to the action to read its words: Austerlitz, Jena, Friedland, Essling and Wagram, proving that this was a battle hardened and formidable enemy. But now they were trying to make a break for it, to get their valued standard back to the safety of their lines. Scott could hear the heavy galloping of Sergeant Ewart's horse and within seconds it had brought the Sergeant into close quarters combat with the six Frenchmen. Scott looked around perplexed; there should have been foot soldiers of the British here. The Gordon Highlanders had fought in this part of the battle. They had been spurred on by the sight of their magnificent cavalry, almost at the end of a day of bloody fighting and still exhausted after fighting over the last few days at nearby locations like Quatre Bras and Charleroi. He had read war memoirs from the 92nd in which they had boasted of hanging onto the cavalry's stirrups as they passed so that they could reach the fighting much quicker, their blood up, wanting vengeance for all their slaughtered comrades. He looked surprised that Ensign Kinchant was still amongst them, still mounted, as Sergeant Ewart slashed through the shoulder of a Frenchman who then fell onto his knees, as his arm dropped macabrely to the ground, allowing the blade to return easily to Sergeant Ewart. With once quick deft movement he then used it to slash through the jaw of the French soldier trying to flee with the Eagle, before bringing it brutally down on his head to finish the mortally wounded man off. As Sergeant Ewart dragged his sabre through the head of his enemy Scott anticipated seeing chips of skull and the greyish redness of the inner mush but instead watched Sergeant Ewart sheathing his sword with ease despite the gore that would have clogged its journey. Scott watched fascinated as new history was being portrayed in front of him. A frown crossed his face as his head shook, there should have been more fighting, more blood, the mercy and betrayal of Ensign Kinchant did not happen. Sergeant Ewart should have taken a French head clean off by now with his light cavalry blade that he had patiently waited in line several hours before the battle at the Regiment's armourer to have sharpened on his turning stone towards the blade's point to create a more effective slashing weapon.

Yet now the Sergeant had dismounted from his horse and was picking up the Eagle, standing in front, in full view of everyone, regardless of the risk of musket fire and the dangers of artillery bombardment, waving it triumphantly in the air like a football fan with a scarf rejoicing at his team's winning goal in the last minutes of an even game. A mounted man, with lots of braid upon his uniform, ordered authoritatively across to him:

'You, brave fellow, take that to the rear,' he pointed to the Eagle that the Sergeant, now with a wide smile across his face, was still waving triumphantly in the air, 'you have done enough till you get quit of it,' he said in the formal language of this 19th Century era, maintaining strict officer decorum despite the heat of battle.

With a nod towards General Pack, his most senior officer, Sergeant Ewart started to wrap the streamers of the banners around his arm and in his haste he stumbled and involuntary ran forward a few steps in an effort to right himself, his scabbard clunking on the ground as it bounced several times. Calum, the actor playing him, then tripped over the stage lighting lamps that backlit the area for the benefit of this now shocked Aberdeen audience, the LED par cans shattered with a sharp crinkle of glass and he fell into the orchestra pit of His Majesty's Theatre with a heavy thump and sharp crack.

Chapter 3

Scott jumped up from his red velvet seat, recognising the sharp crack as the unmistakable sound of a human bone snapping violently, the sudden screaming of the actor before the hushed audience confirming his suspicions. The silent shocked audience started a crescendo of a murmur that slowly turned into a gaggle of gasps as each member looked around them, all were unsure if this was part of the play. Scott wasted no time; he confidently and dutifully realised that his skills would be needed. He too had heard the sickening thump and knew a spinal injury may also have occurred to the unfortunate actor. He turned to his father in the seat to his left, 'I think I'm needed faither.'

'Aye, ma loon,' replied his dad, Douglas, in an equally calm tone, using his North East of Scotland Doric dialect for boy, 'that you will be son,' he replied as he moved his knees to the side, next to the cushioned armrest, so that his son could reach the aisle that he was blocking.

Scott wasted no time, he ignored the screeching of the theatre microphone as it was hastily fumbled by the stage manager in his smart suit, the high pitched feedback tuned out as the entire audience heard: 'Ladies and Gentlemen,' he began as Scott ran down the rake of the aisle, the gradual decline helping his momentum to reach the wounded man. 'Er, please be seated, there is nothing to worry about, just a wee accident,' stammered the nervous manager. Whilst Scott was confidently intent on reaching his new patient, the manager was clearly as shocked as the audience. He was flapping his arms about, pointing to the golden rimmed stage curtain, the front of house tabs that poked out from the ceiling, motioning frantically for the backstage crew to lower the rest of the red velvet material that matched the seats. His thoughts were to save the audience from the aghast faces of the other actors who were peering down into the deep orchestra pit, hidden from view from most of the audience by a red curtain, where the wounded man was now screaming; his blood pumping out onto the immaculate theatre's floor. 'We've everything in hand, please don't panic. I'm afraid we shall have to cancel the show.' His hesitation ceased as he remembered the emergency drills that senior management of the Aberdeen Performing Arts Committee had implemented for just such an emergency. He knew that his first-aid trained usher would be on her way to attend to the injured actor, to make an initial assessment. He also knew that another usher was making his way to the designated first aid room, the old-fashioned original box office, at the front of the theatre steps, to retrieve the theatre's first aid equipment. 'Please be seated whilst we attend to the injured actor.'

There were more murmurs from the audience, no longer shocked, more inquisitive. Some were starting to pull out their mobile phones, selfishly ready to take a video or photo to share on social media to their pals. Others were standing up, macabrely wanting to gain a better view of the wounded man. The front row was also on their feet, jumping about on the pink and red patterned carpet for a better view. They were getting in Scott's way. Some started to walk over to the small curtained-off orchestra pit, peering over the ornate highly polished brass railings that gleamed in the darkened theatre as rays of light bounced around from the stage like a mischievous fairy.

'Oot o the way, ye glakit bams,' he shouted, 'guan back tae yer seats!' Though Scott was roaring this order for his fellow Aberdonians to get back to their seats, in his best parade-ground voice, few paid him any notice. Still running along the space by the front seats now, Scott grabbed one of the mobile phones from a startled youth with daft looking short back and sides but an untidy mop of long spiked up top hair and a bushy beard that resembled an unkempt, startled old man. His phone had been in camera mode and he had been resizing the screen for a close up. Seeing that it was handily turned on and not password protected Scott quickly threw it up to the stage manager as he passed level with him. He caught it instinctively. 'Phone for an ambulance now, and tell me when you've done it,' he commanded the astonished man, not used to being ordered about in his own theatre.

Scott reached the gated area of the orchestra pit at the same time as the designated first aider, a pale looking art student from nearby Gray's School of Art in the nearby neighbourhood of Garthdee, Scott's home area. She was working here at His Majesty's Theatre part time to fund her University degree course materials and was clearly in shock as she fumbled the catch. Scott deftly helped her and sprinted the few feet to the actor who was still on the floor, groaning loudly and helplessly on his back, his left leg looking unnaturally bent and with a clearly seen fragmented white bone projecting over his kneecap, blood was pumping around him, quickly discolouring the bone into a darker red mass. The familiar coppery salty smell assailed Scott's nose as he fought back memories that tried to come rushing back to assault his mind of former incidents that he preferred locked away in a box in his head, with the key thrown away for good measure. And the bare room the box was safely stored in, locked and bolted. Scott saw the violin player, dressed all in black, like a harbinger of doom, gently lay down his instrument onto his chair and then walk towards the actor, intent on helping him. 'Dinnae move him!' screamed Scott.

The violin player momentarily froze, 'I was just going to help him, that's all,' he said indignantly, noticing that bizarrely this stranger before him was unbuckling his belt and slipping it through the loops of his jeans. His words were lost on Scott now that he was passing the speakers and the tannoy system once more crackled back to life.

'Ladies and gentlemen, please do not be alarmed,' begged the actor who had played General Pack. Almost as if in character he now took control of the microphone whilst the stage manager was phoning 999. 'The ushers will now escort you from the building whilst we care for my colleague.' His words fell on deaf ears as the majority of the audience were now on their feet, most were trying to get to the aisles, some intent on reaching the theatre's two bars on their split levels whilst others were trying to get nearer the stage for a better look. Those in the gracefully curved Upper Circles were leaning precariously over the gold coloured protective banisters with their red velvet drapes to try and get a better look at what was going on. They gave no thought to the clever system of patented lifts and cantilevers on the back walls that supported their weight and that of this raised area, a design so ingeniously used for over 80 more theatres that included the Hackney Empire in London and the King's Theatre in Glasgow. Nor did they realise that they had a better view of the stage and what was unfolding in the orchestra pit because this system meant that no supporting pillars, which would have blocked their views, were needed. The more sensible of the audience were making for the exit, knowing that their evening's entertainment was over; some were silently praying that the injured man would be okay. A few old meanies, hoping for a refund, were making for the new box office built in the recent £7.8 million refurbishment glass extension foyer by the café and below the 1906 restaurant which had closed an hour before, their pre-theatre patrons having been well fed on char grilled pork loin with mustard mash, haggis bon bons and pickled vegetables served with cider jus, a particular favourite of Scott's dad, Douglas.

Scott was already kneeling by the patient, mentally running through his emergency first aid procedures taught once more during the Advanced Team Medic refresher training at 22 Field Hospital in Aldershot. He'd definitely contained and took command of the scene. Now he was mentally running through his primary survey using the easy to remember acronym CABCDE. Over the next few months all army personnel would learn these and how to implement them. This would then mean that small sections of soldiers would always have basic first aid should they not have a team Combat Medical Technician with them, particularly useful for small cadres operating in remote foreign locations. Scott quickly muttered their full meanings under his breath, to remind himself of what was required of him, and to help focus his mind, as he quickly unhooked his belt from the last of his stubborn belt hooks and pulled it free with a whipping sound. 'Okay, Catastrophic Haemorrhage, Airway and Cervical Spine Control, Breathing, Circulation with Haemorrhage Control, Disability and Exposure,' he finished muttering as he knelt down by his casualty and slid his leather belt, a present from his late fiancée, just above the left knee of Calum, taking great care not to move the limb, even a fraction. 'Fit like loon?' he asked loudly of the actor who was still screaming, but who was aware enough to interrupt his yelling and say, 'eh?' in return.

'Sorry laddie, I'm too broad sometimes, I was asking you how are you? Try and stay still, this is going to hurt a wee bittie.' Though what Scott was really doing was checking that this man, his new patient, was breathing, conscious and aware. He quickly pulled the belt tight and secured it through one of its holes, ensuring it was held tight and acted adequately as the improvised tourniquet he had intended. Scott ignored the roar of pain that spewed from Calum's mouth along with spittle that danced in the air, almost pirouetting before falling into the actor's eyes as this unexpected explosion of pain attacked his delicate nerve endings that registered this assault and with it a sudden obstruction of blood flow.

'What's your name, I'm guessing it's not Sergeant Ewart!' Scott said as he turned to look the actor in the eyes, seeing them starting to glaze over.

The actor gave a few pants and replied 'Calum,' the ornate ceiling was lost on his blurring gaze.

'Right, Calum, you were bleeding a lot and you've got what we call a compound, sorry, an open fracture of your tibia, your front leg bone is sticking out, that was quite a height you've fell fae,' said Scott, gently, hoping that by talking in a slow rhythm it would help Calum subconsciously slow down his breathing and help him with the pain until the paramedics got here. During this conversation Scott was shuffling over to within Calum's eyesight. 'Now Calum, you still with me, try not to move, and especially don't move your head.'

Calum panted out again and was getting more breathless now as he said, 'Aye, fitiver,' before screaming like a banshee as Scott, seeing more fresh blood pumping out, leant down and tightened his belt, the 'yes, whatever' answer being his cue that Calum was ready. The audience gave a collective ooh, as if this was a performance that they had to react to and encourage the actor to go on with his lines. Only Calum was in a world of pain and unable to perform for them. His forehead was becoming more spotted with beads of sweat and he was looking paler than the usher had initially been and his skin turned clammy. Scott had no time to admire the urns to the side of the Royal and Directors Boxes near to the stage and the marble statue figurines of the goddesses with their ornate 24 carat gold leaf, one of comedy with the lute and the other tragedy holding a sword: though perhaps he'd have wished for their ethereal help had he been a religious man once more. He didn't have much time, or the resources to save Calum.

'So sorry Calum,' said Scott apologetically, 'you were losing vital blood volume and I had to stop you bleeding all over the theatre floor and the only way I could do that was with a tourniquet above your knee, is that okay?' Scott knew the question was irrelevant because it had happened anyway since it was all he had here to use. He wished he had the luxury of an emergency trauma dressing and traction splints. The poor chap would have to grit his teeth and cope best with the pain, certainly no intramuscular or intravenous painkillers, or even the new fentanyl lozenge, to help him, that and the all-important antibiotics would have to wait for the professionals. At least he was free of foreign land dirt and muck to his wound, and neither of them had to dodge bullets. Scott deftly reached down and felt for the man's dorsalis pedal pulse above his toes, miraculously relieved that it was there and that he hadn't had to perform a fracture reduction because this man's neurovascular bundle was still intact – just. If he'd had to do that then this unfortunate man's screams would have been enough to shatter the 1972 water damaged and refurbished London Royal Opera House chandelier that was above them. Despite its 126 light bulbs Scott had difficulty seeing around him since no-one had thought to turn on the lights. He'd been working on the dim light used by the orchestra. It had all happened so quickly, only seconds ago he had been seated by his father enjoying the play during his leave. As if his thoughts had been read, the light switch had been thrown by a stage hand taking instructions from his senior over their walkie talkie system, basking the entire theatre in light.

Looking up Scott was momentarily distracted by the finely modelled frieze of The Goddess of Drama high above the ornate proscenium arch that had been sculpted by William Buchan of nearby Belmont Street, near to the Army Careers Office where Scott had received the metaphorical Queen's Shilling years ago. With the better lighting Scott could now see Peter, the violinist, more closely and saw his fretful look. 'Apologies for shouting mate, but Calum here must not be moved and especially must not move his head, he fell a long way and may have a spinal injury.' Scott checked Peter's reaction and could see that he understood. Okay, what's your name?' he asked quickly of the violin player for he could see that he needed to assess Calum's injuries further. His screaming at least let Scott know that he was still conscious and breathing.

'Oh, yeah. Hi. Er, I'm Peter.'

'Nice tae meet you Peter, great music by the way,' replied Scott wanting to make a quick rapport with the violinist and boost his confidence. 'You can be a great help by kneeling down here and keeping your hands here,' said Scott as he guided Peter's hands whilst he was in mid-crouch to the sides of Calum's head. These delicate hands were more used to the intricate playing of his stringed

25

instrument than holding a stranger's head. 'Please do not allow this man to move his head, he may have injured his back and this will stop any further damage, that okay?' hurried Scott as he nodded his own head, seeking the same affirmation from Peter who was soon nodding vigorously as if beating time to his own musical rhythm. 'Good man,' said Scott as he stood up and walked around to the actor's broken leg, 'You're doing fine Peter, just continue to hold Calum's head like that please, it's just perfect how you are doing.' He looked up to check on Peter again with a nod of his head, who returned the nod quickly.

'What are you doing, how can I help,' blurted the usher quickly in her haste to get the words out, now by Scott's side. She'd stood back watching this stranger plunging straight in to help, a little in awe and mostly afraid, this was her first real life casualty. 'I'm first aid trained and should be doing something,' she pleaded to Scott.

'Good,' said Scott, taking in her smart appearance of burgundy waistcoat, white blouse and black trousers and surmising that she was a theatre usher, 'affa sorry, I seem to have taken charge here lass. I'm Scott; I'm an army trained combat medic, a first aider if you like, and nurse. Where's your first aid gear?' asked Scott, wishing he'd had a field medical pack with him to better treat Calum's injuries.

The Usher looked forlornly up the aisle which was now thronging with folk, unsure what to do and where they had to go. 'I'm the designated first aid responder and my kit is in the first aid room, up there,' she pointed hopelessly as if trying to reach beyond the double doors leading to the old foyer area with her outstretched finger. 'Garry should be bringing it to me, but I'm not sure if he'll safely get past that crowd of folk.'

'Ah, then we have a problem, how are we going to get it… what's your name?'

'Kirsty, it'll take a few minutes to reach with the crowd, it's like a free entrance day at Pittodrie!'

Scott laughed inwardly at the mention to the local football team's stadium, though the circumstances were grim, 'I like your humour Kirsty, though we need help here,' he looked gravely at Calum, who was turning much paler and panting heavier. He whispered to her almost conspiratorially, 'Calum has lost a lot of blood, I was too long in reaching him and getting this tourniquet on,' he pointed to his blood splattered belt, the intricate Celtic patterns no longer discernible. 'Calum is about to go into shock. Then we have big problems, can you deal with this with me, you'll be a big help? I can't do it alone.'

'I, I think so,' said Kirsty, wishing she was back in her art studio, working on her latest canvas, a scenic panorama of local hill Bennachie.

'Good,' said Scott, 'I wish we had some intravenous fluid to give to him. Just remember your training drills Kirsty; because I think Calum is about to go into cardiac arrest, see how pale he is,' replied Scott, still whispering, 'that's a sign of peri-arrest. Where is your defibrillator, I assume a theatre of this size has one?'

'Aye, we do, but...'

'...it's in the first aid room', interrupted Scott with a sigh, looking up at the out of control crowds, despite General Pack's orders, which the actor playing him was vainly shouting through the Public Address system, to no avail. Scott looked up to the stage to see the stage manager who was passing down the mobile phone to the belligerent youth who grabbed it back and started to look around its casing and screen and caress it as if it was a cherished baby being handed back to a new mother after an aging aunt had fawned over it.

'They'll be here in two minutes,' shouted across the stage manager as he straightened up his tie, now ready to assume command of his realm once more.

'What entrance will they be coming to,' shouted Scott back to him, whilst pointing to the main foyer, now heaving with folk trying to exit or reach ushers to ask them questions.

'No, Aberdeen ambulance control ken tae tell them tae come tae the stage door, they can back straight up and come through that door,' he pointed to the emergency exit by the Royal Box, which had been used by the Queen Mother for a Royal Variety performance and by Princess Margaret, the late Colonel in Chief of the Queen Alexandra's Royal Army Nursing Corps, Scott's Corps, who held the position for an incredible 48 years. She had enjoyed the ballet performance of Swan Lake. In later years Prince Charles and Prince Edward, on trips from nearby Balmoral Castle, broke with tradition and sat in the Dress Circles so that they could enjoy better views of the stage.

Scott looked over and was startled to see an elderly gentleman sat in the middle chair, pointing a smart wooden cane with silver top at him. What had made Scott double-take at him was that this man was wearing a smart old-fashioned top hat, silver jacket, frilly shirt cuffs and ruffle down his shirt. He looked so out of place with his shiny tie pin that caused the theatre lighting to bounce around it, but yet he looked completely at home in this renowned Edwardian era building that had been designed by the famous theatre architect Frank Matcham. He even had matching, but greying, handlebar moustache and beard like that worn by King Edward VII, though this man had taken the trouble to wax his moustache so that the edges stuck out like a pointer dog proudly showing its master his retrieved shot and downed prey. He continued to stare at him along the sights of his cane that was as erectly trained on Scott as a far-off sniper finding its mark through his sights.

'You okay Scott?' asked a troubled Kirsty, fearing that this stranger was no longer in control.

'Oh, aye, yes, sorry, I was momentarily distracted,' he glanced quickly away from Kirsty back to the Royal Box, which was now empty. Scott then shook his head to clear it from this odd experience and then looked across to Calum and started to unbutton his heavy red material Waterloo replica tunic, 'are you okay Calum?' he gently enquired.

'Mmmrrraa,' was his only response as his breathing became more shallow but rapid.

Alarm bells started ringing loudly in Scott's ears, though he was deaf to the noise of the audience and tannoy system, trying to direct people away from the theatre for the night. He looked up vainly to where the first aid room was beyond the doors where people were pushing and shoving to get out, 'no chance,' he thought vainly as he saw the ushers futile struggle to create order. He was grateful for the breeze coming from the emergency door to the side of them, but unfairly ungrateful of the time the ambulance was taking to travel the four streets in the few seconds since the 999 call. How he longed for a Guedel airway and ambu-bag, the bag and valve with mask system that aided resuscitation and the all-important defib he just knew he needed to help keep Calum alive until the professionals came. All of these thoughts occurred in just seconds, unlike the minutes that it was taking Garry, the other usher, to slowly make his way against the throng of people, to the orchestra pit with the theatre's substantial first aid kit.

'Shouldn't you be releasing the tourniquet now and again to stop his foot losing blood flow?' questioned Peter, still holding in place Calum's head between his hands and knees of his black trousers that all his fellow musicians wore in an attempt to look invisible and not distract patrons from the play with their musical movements. 'I saw that in a TV programme once.'

'Normally aye Peter, but my experience in Afghanistan and in the aftermath of the Nepal earthquake is that the casualty needs to preserve as much of their own blood as possible to survive,' he pointed to his belt, he knew he'd no longer be able to use that last birthday gift from his beloved before her shocking death months later. He looked away, expunging the dark memories from his mind; he had a life to save, and this time he would be successful. He wished he had a cannula so that he could insert it into a vein of Calum's before he shut down. What would he have given for an 18-gauge saline lock and intravenous fluid, preferably plasma expander to try and compensate for the blood loss? He knew there was no point in such stupid thoughts or feeble prayers; there was no higher being to help him. He felt for Calum's carotid pulse, just to the side of his windpipe, it was weak and growing weaker with each vital second. 'Stay with me Calum, I want to see how your play ends when your leg heals. I also want to tell you all where you went wrong in your re-enactment.' There was no response from Calum from this deliberate goading from Scott. He was now cold to the touch and was sweating under the glare of the hot theatre lights, though they were not the cause. Scott turned to Kirsty who nervously ran her fingers through her bushy hair and then wiped them on her black trousers. 'How have you been taught Cardiopulmonary resuscitation lass?'

'Oh, the standard one through the Red Cross courses,' gasped Kirsty, 'I've never done it on a real person before, only the big dolls,' she replied fretfully. 'That's okay, we'll help each other, Calum's about to go into cardiac arrest, his pulse is weakening, we've no heart monitor but I can tell from his signs.' He looked up to the door, he tried focusing his mind, but could faintly hear a rubidub dum reverberation, a sound that had been growing louder these last few weeks, almost as if he was conscious of his own heartbeat echoing around his body. He pushed these thoughts aside, he needed to appear in control to Kirsty and Peter if he needed their help.' Okay, so you know how to do chest compressions when Calum's heart stops working?'

Kirsty started to unbutton her smart deep burgundy waistcoat, 'Aye and rescue breaths,' she added helpfully, physically and mentally preparing herself for her important task.

'Grand,' replied Scott, he felt for Calum's pulse, 'och, no,' he exclaimed as he withdrew his fingers. 'He's gone, we need to get to work, and fast.' He looked up at Peter, 'That's been a great help mate, but now his breathing takes priority, so let me in about, and gently release his head and go back to your seat. Peter did as he was told, not even thinking of questioning Scott who was now leaning his cheek over Calum to check if he was breathing. He instinctively opened Peter's mouth and ascertained that there was nothing in it, nor that there was any foreign object or vomit at the back of his throat. Scott looked up at the ashen faced stage manager who took a tentative step forward to the rim of the stage to the gaps between the lights. Reaching into his pocket Scott pulled out his mobile phone and threw it up the few feet to the manager, grateful that he caught it because it contained valuable photos of his lover who was no longer with him. Only then did he notice that the advertising curtain with ads for websites and services like aboutaberdeen.com with a funny bagpipe cartoon logo had been pulled down instead of the heavy velvet material curtain. His unconscious mind registered that the actors, their props, replica weapons and the large sturdy horse models had been removed whilst he had been working on Calum. 'Call 999 again and tell them that he is no longer breathing and that he has no pulse. Tell them to inform A&E that an unresponsive patient is coming and ask for an ETA on the ambulance crew. Tell them I'm an army nurse and have stopped the bleeding with an improvised tourniquet and am starting chest compressions and rescue breaths along with Kirsty's help.'

Kirsty, no longer the frightened usher, but now a veteran blooded first aider, was now knelt down by Calum's chest, feeling part of a team, confidently ready to help save her first life. She had already placed the heel of her hand over Calum's sternum and had interlocked her hands, ready to press down with life-saving artificial pumping, just as she had been taught. 'You're doing great Kirsty, looks like you had a great teacher,' said Scott encouragingly, 'I need you to perform 30 of those, counting out loudly.' She obeyed and started her counting, pressing up and down, she kept her hands locked in position on Calum the whole time. 'Great Kirsty, you really are doing well.'

'25, 26, 27, 28, 29, 30,' said a breathless Kirsty, surprised at the exertion needed to maintain the blood pumping around Calum's organs, hoping to keep him alive. She continued talking as Scott gently tilted Calum's head back by about an inch, the possible spinal damage no longer the top priority now that he wasn't breathing or had a pulse. Scott then pinched Calum's nose as he simultaneously sealed his mouth over Calum's open sagging mouth and formed as tight a seal as he could so no valuable air could escape. As his eyes roamed down to Calum's naked chest he exhaled into Calum's mouth the valuable air needed to reach his lungs and was satisfied to see his chest rise. Scott repeated the procedure and moved his head back and nodded back to Kirsty who was already counting with each chest compression. Both continued this practice like a well-rehearsed ballet performance, the only sounds were Kirsty's confident counting out aloud as she tried to maintain a rate of between 100 and 120 a minute despite her aching shoulders and Scott's deep vital breaths shared to Calum.

During their third repetition Scott looked up to see his dad waving encouragingly to him with a big thumbs up, all this time he had remained quietly watching his son proudly from his seat in the Dress Circle. He'd never seen his son 'at work' before. He knew that he had a difficult job, that he had battled personal trauma from his head injuries and even inner psychological demons, from the cries that woke their neighbours penetrating through the thick granite walls in the middle of the night as he was reliving that fateful day that took away his sweetheart so violently.

But 'Michty me!' Douglas thought, 'fit a braw loon!' his heart was humbled. As the theatre finally emptied of its patrons, the first aid kit was brought to Scott by a sweating apologetic looking usher. Simultaneously the ambulance crew burst through the side door, their flashing blue light showing up their perfectly reversed vehicle with each rhythmic strobe, its doors were left ajar, ready to whisk off their casualty in their wheeled stretcher. Scott envied them the defibrillator and huge medical pack that they carried; wishing he'd had those minutes earlier. He was grateful that he hadn't the worry of prolonged field care to give to Calum. During their efforts he was running through his head the "HITMAN" all-over body-check now taught to CMTs to be performed after the primary survey and immediate treatment. This stood for Hydration and Heat, Infection, Tubes, Medication, Analgesia and Nutrition and Nursing. Scott had heard stories, over coffee breaks, of army medics being sued by ungrateful civilians after life-saving efforts before the NHS paramedics could get there. He'd always thought these to be urban myths since no-one in The Hub could regale him with exact examples of litigation, besides, what type of person sues the person who just saved your life?

'You'll have to leave the theatre now sir,' said another usher, immaculate in her uniform despite her ordeal in trying to make everyone in the audience leave the building in an orderly fashion. She noticed the man was gently wiping away tears from his eyes with a paper tissue. 'It's been an affa nicht, hasn't it, shocking to see,' she said to the gentleman.

'Aye,' replied Douglas, straightening up in his chair. 'That's ma loon doon there, saving that man's life. His mither would have been proud of him.'

'Oh, sorry, is your wife no longer with us?' the usher gently enquired, wondering if this recent bereavement was the cause of the man's tears amid this heightened emotional night.

'No, cancer te'en her awa fae us, she was a wonderful lass, she'd have been michty proud of our loon. An here's me greeting away like a bairn when he's so brave fighting our wars, nursing our troops and still saving folk.'

'It takes a brave man to show his emotions too, your wife and son wouldnae mind you crying. I'm supposed to make sure all our customers have gone and you're the last one here. I'll get into trouble if I leave you here, but...'

Sensing her dilemma Douglas patted her upper arm and said thoughtfully, 'Nae bither quine, could you tell ma loon I'll meet him in the Noose and Monkey, I can do with a drink aifter a this.'

The quine, the girl, nodded encouragingly at the older man, 'thank you, I could dee with ane maself! I just hope the actor will be alright. Your son looks like he ken's fit he's deein.'

'Aye, he does that lass, he does that,' said Douglas as he got proudly to his feet. He allowed his chair seat to fall back to the upright position quietly and then made his way to the exit.

'6, 7, 8..' continued Kirsty, her exertions starting to slow down with fatigue, relieved that she could see the paramedics in their green uniforms coming towards them, pushing a trolley laden with medical gear.

'Okay, what have we got?' asked the leading paramedic, her partner already unbuckling the large haversack and pulling out vital equipment from various pockets, his expert eyes already having taken in the patient's needs. She brushed her long black fringe out of her eyes.

Scott was momentarily taken aback, his mind whirling back to another green clad medic, to a time when she was handing over to him a patient, remembering the same instinctive hair and hand movement of a past love.

'Hello, sunshine, did you hear me? I'm Yvonne, I'll take over now, but please quickly let me know what's been going on, are you the army nurse dispatch told us were treating the patient, what's happened?'

'Sorry, it's been quite a nicht,' replied Scott, focusing his mind, 'Aye, I'm Scott, this is Kirsty, the theatre's first aider,' he said nodding down to Kirsty who was continuing the vital chest pumping. 'The loon's Calum, he's an actor who fell fae the stage tae here, Peter, the violinist, kept him immobile while I arrested the bleeding with a tourniquet, my belt, as you can see.' Scott and

Yvonne both looked down to Calum's whitening foot in sharp contrast to the congealed red floor and bloodied pulp mixture of bone, muscles and fat drying out now that none of his vital fluids were flowing and ebbing out of him. 'I've checked his neurovascular bundle after the belt was applied, and found it intact. No reduction was needed.'

Yvonne looked up, impressed by this stranger who had done all the right things to save this man's life and surprised that he even knew how to safely perform a fracture reduction had it have been needed.

'He went into arrest soon after, so Kirsty and I have been performing CPR until you got here, seven cycles of 30 to 2 so far.'

'Brilliant, thank you…'

'Scott, Scott Grey, I'd say pleased to meet you, but I ken you'll get busy now. So I'll leave you experts to it.'

'Aye,' she replied as she checked Calum's airway, continuing her conversation with Scott as she delved into the bag, that her fellow paramedic Bill had taken and placed to her side. He was already laden with kit and had checked the tourniquet and was quickly putting on defibrillator and heart monitoring pads onto Calum's chest. 'Thanks Scott you've done well, you and Kirsty and Peter,' she said turning around to smile warmly at Kirsty, who was being helped to her feet with the paternal help of the theatre manager, his huge hands already wrapping themselves around her for reassurance and support due to her jelly-like legs that were also stiff from her exertions. Peter was long gone with the rest of the orchestra, back to the green room for tea and biscuits to steady their nerves. 'I'm Yvonne,' she said as she turned around to give Scott a reassuring smile too, 'Bill and I will take over now, thanks.' With one last smile to Scott she looked away and started to work on Calum with Bill, each movement carefully choreographed through years of training and experience finely honed on the streets of Aberdeen.

Scott stood up, took a few steps backwards and almost tripped on an usher who was walking purposely towards him, 'Ah, sorry lass,' he said as the familiar post-adrenaline surge shakes started to affect his body. He took a few deep breaths, remembering the mindfulness training techniques taught to also help him overcome panic attacks, as she ground to a halt in front of him. He turned to face her.

'Nae bither, I just wanted tae tell you that your dad says to meet you at the Noose and Monkey up the road,' she pointed in its general direction, though Scott knew it well, it was a regular haunt of theirs. 'Will he be alright?' she asked pointing over to Calum.

'Aye, he's in the best of hands. Thank you, lass, I'll away and join dad,' sighed Scott to the usher who was already making her way to check on her friend. He looked down and back to the orchestra pit to see that an airway had already been inserted and that Yvonne was shouting 'clear,' and checking around her. She so reminded him of…but then his thoughts and vision were distracted by the man with the silver topped wooden cane again. Only this time his smart suited arm was projecting through the advertising bannered curtain as the cane was once more upstretched directly in Scott's direction. Scott looked incredulously as the man walked right through the thick wooden curtain, not damaging any of the painted adverts, as his body marched easily right through it, took a few steps onto the stage, and with a twinkle of his eyes looked directly at Scott, tucked his cane under his arm and clapped at Scott. This spirit then put his right hand to his top hat, took it off and with a flourish bent over bowing with it held out, as if honouring Scott for a job well done, for the best performance of the night. The old-fashioned gentleman then straightened, tweaked his waxed moustache, brought down his cane to steady his posture and maintain his balance, and then vanished before Scott's amazed eyes, as if a trap door had immediately swallowed him into the bowels of the hungry stage.

'Are you alright son?' asked a man who appeared at Scott's side. He wore a knotted scarf around his neck, white collarless shirt, light brown dustcoat, brown trousers and boots, and spoke in a broad Aberdonian accent, 'you look like you've just seen a ghost!'

Chapter 4

'I rather think I have,' replied a puzzled and dazed Scott. He looked around to see if he could find the well-dressed old-fashioned man to no avail. He had simply vanished into thin air, like a well entertained patron rushing home to bed.

Taking Scott's unusual response in his stride, the newcomer took Scott gently by the elbow, leading him away from the medics working away to save their new patient. 'Come away and get cleaned up ma loon, you've a bittie of blood about you and if you dinnae mind me saying you're a bit sweaty too. I'm a stagehand here. Look, I'll take you back through to where you can get cleaned up. You'll feel better after a wash, then you can join your dad a bit more respectable looking, like, for that well-deserved drink.'

Only now did Scott take the time to look at his purple red blood encrusted hands. They shook slightly as he knew that they would since he was still recovering from the adrenaline shakes and what he knew to have been a ghostly encounter, just like the Grey Lady said he should expect more of. Scott let himself be led up the steps to the stage. He followed the newcomer through to the right, past lots of panels of switches and tall speakers, taking care of the jumble of trailing wires that looked like heaped spaghetti on a plate that scattered the side of the stage. He ignored the painted backdrop of a Belgian field covered in white plumes of gun smoke at the rear of the stage, what had been the background scenery to tonight's initial drama, and followed the man down several wooden steps and into a white painted bricked corridor with red heavy linoleum type flooring. The front of house glitz and glamour was no longer in evidence here behind the scenes where stagehands, wardrobe, makeup and many others worked seamlessly to help to create the magic of theatre for their nightly and Saturday matinee audiences. All the while, as he followed the stagehand, Scott was wondering what the ghostly top hatted gentleman had wanted. It certainly was not to be laid to rest like Jim at Erskine Nursing Home, who had just wanted peace from his lifetime of needless guilt. Was this phantom merely watching over Scott or simply congratulating him on a job well done? Scott knew that like many theatre's, HMT was supposed to be heavily haunted by several spirits, such as Miss Mitchell who was said to walk the foyer. Many who had seen her elderly ethereal form walk through the building had thought she was on her way to work in death, as in life, in the Stalls Bar. His dad would have joked that even with her; the interval drinks wouldn't have got served any quicker! Whatever the old-fashioned gentleman had wanted, Scott had felt no fear from him, unlike in the earliest manifestations of the Grey Lady at his flat in Aldershot built on the old army hospital, the Cambridge Military Hospital. Man, but she had frightened him! This old gentleman had seemed mischievous and sporting. On any other occasion, Scott may even have found him amusing, ghost or no ghost. It was a bit rude really, vanishing quickly and disappearing like that. Perhaps he would reveal himself again later and his questions would be answered. Scott's thoughts soon returned to the stagehand ahead of him who was walking much faster, whistling away tunelessly, almost as if he had forgotten about Scott, away in a world of his own. Scott wondered if any superstitious actors were hearing this broken taboo of the theatre, where mentioning the proper name of the Scottish play by Shakespeare and whistling were considered bad luck for performances. He wryly wondered if he would be frogmarched out of the theatre building, told to spin around on the spot three times, spit on the ground, curse – something Scott hated to do, and then knock on the main door and have to ask to be allowed back in. Totally daft to anyone out-with the theatre profession, though its roots were in tragic and untimely deaths in early 17th productions of Macbeth, but apparently this routine still went on amongst modern thespians treading the boards. The whistling superstition harked back to the days when sailors on shore leave earned an extra crust by operating the rigging system of theatrical props and curtains and would communicate by whistling to each other. Wrong orders were mistakenly given or misunderstood if someone was idly whistling nearby that had in the past resulted in injury and death.

Unconcerned about all this, the stagehand continued to lead, always just out of gain, forcing Scott to follow like an obedient old wee dog after its too fast master during their evening walk together. They delved further back to the depths of the inner workings of the theatre, where some would say that the real work took place. He passed the steamy laundry room where emissions of smoke filled the air and he saw that several women, each of whom were dressed in matching pinafores with front pockets and wearing scarves over their hair, were looking as sweaty as he was. They were hand-washing garments in adjoining sinks, before wringing them out and folding them into laundry baskets. Scott wondered why the man wasn't leading him to these sinks where one was vacant, and part of him wondered why Aberdeen's leading theatre did not have washing machines and tumble driers. He almost had to run to keep up with the man, and as he did so he saw him move past a group of similarly dressed men, though some had long brown overalls with deep pockets at the front, just to the sides of their large buttons that secured the garment but still allowed their shirts and neck scarves to be seen. Two were taking turns to rotate a cumbersome handle on an old hoisting machine that turned and lifted a platform beside a high bricked wall in which two jet black horses stood. Only, unlike those on the stage, these animals were very much alive and were being kept in check by another stagehand, his tackety boots sparking on the metal platform as he dug his heels in to steady his nervous equestrian cargo. They were making their way reluctantly to the stage area, higher up, on this hoist designed for a cargo of sets and heavy props. With one hand on their reins and the other motioning the others upwards he shouted out 'up a bittie more laddies,' to his workmates further below.

Scott was distracted by his familiar looking stagehand. He was still out of reach ahead of him and had climbed down the stairs on the opposite walkway to an observation platform where he was leaning over the banister for a better look at the horses above him. He shook his head as if in disagreement with what was going on around him, stood back, turned and made his way down to the winching stagehands. Scott moved forward, working out how to reach his guide a bit sooner but saw that he was already with his work friends. He was helping them by applying the brake in an effort to halt the hoist safely and to calm down the movements of the winching mechanism. As he did so the wound up hoist gained momentum and the winch men were unable to control its sudden descent, 'LOOK OUT!' screamed Scott in warning, foreseeing what was playing before him. As the stagehand who he had tried to keep up with looked to Scott, the hoist and its overburdened cargo sped downwards and towards him. He tried leaning further forward to gain a better view just as the winch handle flew loose from its mechanism and the grasp of the other workmen who were unable to safely hold it. With a grinding and jarring of metal it flew forwards off its holdings at great speed and with a sickening squelch took his head clean off. His body stayed upright for a ghastly second, then swayed left and right before it buckled like a rag doll and toppled over the safety banister. Blood sprayed the horses as pieces of bone and grey brain matter whipped across to their shocked handler who was momentarily stunned by what he was helplessly witnessing. He then became blinded by the blood and gore that splattered across his face, forcing its way into his opened eyes and mouth. He lost control of the horses as they neighed and whinnied with fright. The animals snorted heavily in terror and became panicky as they furiously went up onto their hind legs and trampled their front hooves back down in unison several times. More sparks were flying as hooves rubbed against the metal dais flooring as they struggled to maintain a steady grip. The unfortunate stagehand's head, still trailing pulsating nerves and writhing bloody ruptured vessels that squirmed madly like multi-coloured worms trying to escape a fisherman's bait box, landed on the dais with resounding thumps as it bounced twice before stopping motionless. The horses in their struggle then kicked it macabrely on its way across to Scott as if in a horrific game of football on the aftermath of a gory battlefield. Just like the stage manager earlier with the mobiles, Scott instinctively caught the head, his hands clasping it between its ears; its expression looked in mid blink. In disbelief he held it out in front of him as if to get a better look at his prize; he had laid hands on much worse he thought wryly. Unsure of what to do, he wondered just how this night could get any worse. As he asked this to himself it was as if the bodiless head's brain was still functioning and was answering his question telepathically; it turned its now fully opened eyes, looked up to Scott and winked mischievously with a sly grin upon its animated face as a throatless nefarious laugh resounded from its lips and echoed around the building.

Chapter 5

'Dinnae drap ma heid noo loon!' joked the stagehand to a horrified looking Scott who was too stunned to take in the Doric for do not drop my head now boy. 'Ah'm a handsome laddie and dinnae want a black eye, or worse,' the stagehand continued to joke to a bewildered Scott who still held the head aghast at arm's length.

'What the f...what's happening, you're not real are you, you're another ghost! No wonder you weren't concerned about the man going through the stage. You saw him too, didn't you? He's one of you. So were all those ladies in the old steamy, the wash room, and the men in their hob-nailed boots doing the winching and helping with the horses. You are all phantoms!' shouted Scott.

'Aye, sorry loon,' said the stagehand, his mouth still making laughing movements. 'I get bored and fancy a laugh now and again. I kent you could take a better joke than me creaking and groaning my way around in my old building or placing tools elsewhere. Even Savage the Alsatian guard dog had nae sense o humour. I walked beside him and his security guard owner finiver he did their patrol around the Lambeth Walk.' His eyes darted left, as if trying to point out the dark, dingy corridor that ran from the Balcony along the back of the Fly Room down to the Church Lane. It was always cold there, many describing it as near to freezing, even if the heating was full on throughout the theatre.

'I saw how well you handled the puir wee mannie that fell aff the stage, you didnae even retch at the sight of all that blood and the bone sticking oot. Ye did affa well loon,' continued the stagehand, now smiling up at Scott.

Scott relaxed his natural fear a bit, he was now not as angry, but was starting to see the funny side of a big burly security guard, hired by the contractors, Taylor Woodrow, to secure and guard the building and their expensive heavy machinery and tools, during the 1980 to 1982 renovation work, being afraid in this lovely old building. He could just picture the butch guard and his big German Shepherd dog making their way along the walkway with this unseen furtive stagehand creeping up behind them like a tippy-toed ghost in a Scooby Doo cartoon.

Scott still held the head outstretched, but now raised it up to eye level for a better look, surprised by the weight of it. He was equally astonished that no blood was dripping from it onto the floor.

'Oohhhuppp!' chortled the head at that moment, 'mind noo, I cannae abide heights!'

Scott brought the head closer to his eye level, now that he was no longer concerned about getting blood on his trainers and jeans. 'Ye wee… fit makes ye think I winnae play fitba wi yer heid aifter a that?' he said, still angry, but not quite irate. He was also surprised at just how well he was taking this odd encounter. The head smiled back at him, and winked again, to Scott's furiousness. 'I was the striker for Harlaw Academy under 15's in my day ye wee…' he said as he feigned bringing his foot up as if to boot the head like a footballer.

'Ah come on min, that was michty fine fun, best laugh I've had for decades!' he chuckled before seeing the anger in Scott's eyes replace his fear. 'Now, are you gonnae put me back on my shoulders?' requested the stagehand as his eyes kept crossing over to his left, where his headless torso was struggling, getting up onto his knees, trying to right itself blindly. The horses and other phantoms had long gone; unharmed by their fall, saved by this stagehand's use of the brake in death a few moments ago as in life decades ago. Now they were just memories in these old dusty walls, long gone like so many performances blending into the mists of time leaving behind their creative auras. His torso, which was now on its feet, had its arms outstretched like that of a film Frankenstein, though, of course, he was the doctor, not the monster. It was reaching about it blindly, feeling his way down the steps, grasping tightly to the railings; it was drawn instinctively to his head. His tackety boots were making huge reverberating sounds in the emptiness of the backstage area. It was heavy footed like a soldier stamping to attention during a passing out parade. Only it carried on as if marching before coming to rest in front of Scott, who couldn't resist an inquisitive look down its empty neck. He was disappointed to see nothing but hollowness; there weren't even vertebrae to be seen. 'Come on min, gie a loon some privacy,' the head begged as his torso outstretched his arms and surprisingly gently took his head from Scott. 'What did you expect, straw like in Worzel Gummidge or a bright orange incandescent light like in Highlander or the transferring life force as in Doctor Who? I've watched them all along with resting actors in the Green Room over the years. My favourite actors were the Scotland the What? team. Affa funny loons they were. How I miss the company of Stephen Robertson, George Donald and Buff Hardie. Even their producer, James Logan, was funny at times. Nae like those ones on the telly. Yon Christopher Lambert cannae do a guid Scots accent, mind you Peter Capaldi makes a fine Doctor Who and kept his accent, nae like David...'

'I ken fa you are,' interrupted Scott, 'you're Jake! Jake the ghost! Give us a minute, aye got it, John Murray, kent as Jake by a'body, the most famous of Aberdeen ghosts.'

During this unusual conversation Jake had taken the chance to put his head back onto his torso. Scott had watched all the time, fascinated to see if it made a clunk-click sound as it secured tight, like a spaceman's airtight helmet. 'That's me!' Jake the stagehand replied once bodily-whole again. 'I didnae really like John, so a'body called me Jake. Now all the nervous living folk tell me to behave when they are working late and alone, though I still like to move the odd tool or paintbrush, like I'm letting them know that I can be of help. I stay here to look after the old girl; I love this place. I dinnae mean ony harm, most of the creaking and groaning was from the old rope hemp flying system before they replaced it with yon electronic controlled wizardry. A push of the button isnae as romantic to us auld stagehands. And I'm helpful too. When Edi Swann took ill a few years ago, he was on his own, painting away. I helped him oot o the locked door so that he could use the back exit to get to Casualty across the road. Though Bert Ewen, the stage manager, swore blind that he had secured the chain and padlock, he was affa meticulous and I think I dented his pride and reputation.'

'Fit Casualty department across the road?' asked an incredulous Scott, still not believing all he'd seen.

'O'er at Woolmanhill, just across the road from the back exit your fancy ambulance came to, it used to be the main hospital for Aberdeen, afore they built yon new-fangled Aberdeen Royal Infirmary up at Foresterhill, that Miss Mitchell telt me aboot when she joined me. The stuck up cow disnae spik tae me o'er much noo. She thinks front of house staff are michty high and shouldnae spik tae us back-stage boys. Though the spirits o'er there in the new apartments gie me a wave no and then,' said Jake, pointing across to the tall bricked wall.

'No wonder, she doesn't speak to him now,' thought Scott, 'she probably got fed up with his practical jokes.' He was pondering whether to ask him about the spirits over there, in the old hospital building, but thought better of it. Did he really need another Grey Lady in his life? Best to ignore Jake's comment, thought Scott, I've seen enough ghosts for one night. Anymore might tip me over the edge. He instead concentrated on his breathing techniques, this was all normal for him from now on he thought, talking to heads and seeing a headless corpse casually walk along and get its property back. And he would have to keep his new gifts as a secret. If he shared them with the living they'd think him insane and take him to one of the psychiatric wards at Royal Cornhill Hospital and section him. He sadly knew that he was on his own now. 'Is that how you died,' he asked Jake. 'Did you want to share that with me before I help your soul to rest?'

'Aye,' replied Jake, 'in 1942, a muckle World War was going on, our second big one, another war to end all wars, an the heid chiefs' o the theatre decide tae host a Circus. Fitiver next! But dinnae worry about my soul laddie, I'm well happy here.'

'Were you not serving in the military then in 1942?' enquired Scott, remembering that the Grey Lady had told him that his unique gift was to let their story be told, help them seek peace and resolution and then lay these military ghosts to rest.

'Naw laddie, I was o'er auld. I was in ma fifties. Though I was proud when Peter John Donald, the new owner volunteered and was commissioned at the outbreak. He'd done a great job looking after the auld place fae his faither. His brother, James Riddell Donald took o'er when he was fighting an he did a guid job too, looking after the old girl. Besides I'd done ma bittie for King and Country. I was with the other 50,000 Gordon Highlanders who had seen too much awful action in the months of the Battle of the Somme. Over half of us were killed or wounded. I was so lucky to survive without so much as a scratch. Naw, I like it here fine enough, nice and peaceful.'

Scott recalled reading about the Somme Offensive which took place 100 years ago this year and stretched from the 1st July and didn't end until the 18th of November in 1916. Whilst Waterloo saw the British with German allies fight against the French, the Somme now saw the French allied with the British in brutal warfare against Germany over 15 miles of French land. 19,240 British troops died on the first day of the Offensive. One hundred and forty-one days later the British had only seven miles of an advance and never broke the German defence.

'You must have lost lots of mates then?' quizzed Scott, hoping to learn more about this spirit and draw out from him why his troubled soul was still earthbound.

'Aye, too many, too many by far,' replied a rueful Jake, now deadly serious. 'I was in my mid-twenties, so I'd had a wee bittie o a life, but some of the laddies, well they were mair bairns really, they were too young to die, an affa waste. Their puir mithers, how they must have wept at their losses.' At this Jake looked down, crestfallen; all humour gone as he sadly shook his head to reinforce his feelings.

Scott latched onto this last comment and mentally added up Jake's age and that of what his mother may have been when he died so tragically. The sums didn't add up and surely she'd be well dead by now? He thought he'd ask the question anyway in case he was missing something, after all he was still new to this and Jake was only the third ghost he'd had any conversation with. Scott grimaced at the thought that speaking to the dead should become easy and commonplace to him. 'Ah, is that why you're still here; is it your own mother?'

'Naw, laddie, ma mither was well deid afore I went, yon stupid metalwork must have made a richt mess o me. I was glad she didnae see ma body aifter a that,' replied Jake to a confused Scott.

'So is it your guilt over the young lives lost at war? Is that why you are still here, haunting this theatre?'

Jake laughed again, 'Sorry loon, I ken that war is war, lives will be lost, it was brutal and violent, but none of us had time to care about guilt over the others. Sorrowful aye, but nae guilty. We didnae plunge the bayonet and fire the bullet that took their lives. Some of us, me included, did feel guilty about taking the German's lives though. But deep down we knew we were just doing our duty, following orders, letting others make the important decisions. We had some great leaders, our commanders trusted us to do our duty, and we trusted them to lead us. We all kent our duty, even the youngsters. They did all us Gordons proud.'

Scott scratched his head as if showing Jake his confusion. 'So why don't you move on?' Scott looked around him; the backstage of the theatre was now empty. He wasn't even sure what era he was in and could find no signs pointing out a clue to the year. 'Move on then Jake,' instructed Scott looking around for a guiding light, 'time to let go and find your peace.'

Jake laughed, not a raucous outburst like earlier when he had played his prank and showed Scott how he had lost his head, but a nice friendly chuckle. 'No laddie, I'm nay one for moving on. This is ma bonnie theatre and I'm here to look after the auld girl. I may not cause as much mischief as I did years ago, but I do look out for the building and those in it. I'm mair than happy ma loon. I still have the odd laugh, like when the Prince of Wales came on the stage on the 17th of September 1982 to declare the old girl open after her refurbishment. It was me that caused the riser mike to jam. The crew had to go back to the old push up by hand system rather than their fancy new pulley system. But you,' he started to say, looking deep into Scott, as if trying to reach his soul, 'you need some help I'm sensing. You can hear it can't you, the rubidub dum, pounding away in yer heid, nicht aifter nicht?'

'Aye,' replied a puzzled Scott, 'night times are the worst, though I'm hearing it more and more during the day now. Do you ken fit it is?' begged Scott, hoping for an answer to his troubled sleep and the noise that was starting to invade his days.

'It's the start of a new chapter in your life ma loon, a beautiful new chapter,' replied Jake as he drew up his hand, 'you're not blessed with the touch of us, just the sight o us, and I'm an affa sicht for sure. But if I could shake your hand I would. You are going to see some sichts for sure, and lay some of us to rest.

They'll welcome you being their voice in death. But not all will go willingly; some have evil in their hearts, just as they did in life. Cruel, vindictive evil. These you have to be careful of, they will mean you and others harm. Take care ma loon, and accept all the help you get. Now I'm awa tae check on my auld girl and make sure the staff have locked her up. It was affa guid tae meet you loon, affa guid.' With that, Jake turned around and walked down the corridor, his tackety boots echoing around the old deserted building. Breaking more theatre taboos again, he began to whistle the tune to the Cock o' the North, the Gordon Highlanders march, named after the nickname of the Chief of the Gordon clan, Alexander Gordon, the 4th Duke of Gordon, who raised the 92nd Regiment of Foot, The Gordon Highlander, in 1794. As his footsteps receded, Scott could faintly hear Jake start the first bars of Hielan' Laddie, which would have been the official march in his day. In a few seconds Jake was gone, though Scott knew others would still feel his presence for years to come.

Scott waited a respectful minute before turning around and was shocked to see someone from his past, someone long gone, standing right before him with the most beautiful smile and loving gleam in her eyes. She was someone long dead, someone he had yearned to see but had come to accept that he never would. It was someone whose name could still bring him to floods of tears and wrench his heart and twist his stomach at the sheer pain from his loss. She was stood right before him, her disruptive pattern combat jacket and trousers and light brown boots accentuating her diminutive figure.

'Well you fucked that one up, didn't you, haggis muncher!' she said as her merry laughter echoed around the empty building.

An incredulous Scott, who had turned pale, had felt the blood drain from his body from his head down and felt his legs wobble despite all he had experienced this strange night, croaked out a heartfelt and disbelieving 'Naomi?'

Chapter 6

'NO!' bellowed Scott, his roar echoing around the grand old building, amplifying his fury like the battle cry of a Highland Chieftain to his clan. 'NO. NO, NO! You're not here, you're dead. The Taliban blew you up. You're dead, you hear me, YOU, ARE, DEAD. Dead, dead, dead,' Scott kept repeating the words as if this mantra would banish this spirit of his dead fiancée. He screwed up his eyes, trying hard to make himself blind to what he knew was before him, of whom was before him. Part of him wanted to give in to the image, to the dream, to the phantasy and reach out and engulf her, to wrap himself tight around her and bury himself inside of her. To harvest the comfort he so yearned.

'You can't be here: you left with the 453, Hugh and Morag, the Grey Lady. Stop messing with my head. I'm all better now. I don't imagine things, I'm not crazy, I am learning to live with my Post Traumatic Stress Disorder and my head injury. I do my mental exercises, take my medicines, keep myself busy, in shape and eat well. I'm even sleeping better now. 'YOU, ARE, NOT, HERE. LEAVE!' he shouted. Though he commanded her like an adult, he looked like a child, standing there with his eyes tightly shut, tears streaming down his cheeks, dropping heavily to the dusty floor like raindrops during a tempestuous storm.

Naomi reached out to him, unseen by him, and tried to wipe the torrent of tears from his face, her ethereal hands unable to touch her former lover, her best friend and companion. She no longer had a smile on her face, but a look of consternation, furrows formed at her brows as she tried to physically show her worry for her fiancé, the man she had, in life, looked forward to marrying. 'Scott, darling Scott, it really is me. Please look at me. I love you.'

'NO!' roared Scott as his words thundered around the building like the sudden clashing of cymbals. He opened his eyes and looked directly at Naomi. She took a step backwards at the rage she saw in his usually gentle eyes. 'You were blown apart, bits of you were scattered across that god forsaken country. There was very little left to bury. You have passed over. BEGONE,' he ordered her. 'Spirit, I order you begone.'

'No, Scott, no. I really am here, it's me, Naomi,' this new spirit pleaded.

'NO! You cannot be here. You have passed over. You are at peace.' Scott looked at her pleadingly, his eyes had softened and his voice lowered to barely a whisper between heaving sobs. He wanted to reach forward and cup her silky face in his hands, to feel her soft skin, to gain comfort from her warmth. 'I have to believe that you are at peace. I can't lose you again; I can't see you die again. Please spirit, why torment me with the face of her, the only woman I have really loved. Are you the evil that Jake spoke of? This is the worst sort of punishment. I have tried to help the spirits. I have made use of my gift, I helped Jim at Erskine. I tried helping Jake. I've told no-one of this accursed gift. I have listened and helped the spirits move on. Why torment me so?' begged Scott. He remained frozen to the spot, not out of fear, but through sheer disbelief. He put his hands to his face to try to hide the shame he felt at the outpouring of tears and violent, shuddering sobbing that engulfed and surprised him. He sank down, squatting, almost to a foetal position, as if trying to gain the comfort and protection of being back in his mother's womb.

'Oh darling, I am not tormenting you, I love you,' replied Naomi, unable to provide the comfort she yearned to give, 'I have always loved you, in life and in death. I am here to help you, I'm your...'

'NO!' screamed Scott as he looked up, his anger and rage replacing his tears. Spittle flew from his lips as he screamed at her, 'You are an evil abomination, a shape changer, an aberration, a malevolent shapeshifter, a demon. You are all of these things and more...BUT YOU ARE NOT HER! I will not listen to you and order you to leave this realm.'

'No, Scott, no, please listen to me, we need to talk...' began Naomi.

'I don't know what you are, or what you want, but I will not listen to you. If you will not leave, then I must.' Gathering himself and his thoughts together, Scott stood erect and breathed in deeply. 'I have come to terms with my loss. My beloved Naomi is dead and at peace. Nothing can harm her now. I loved her with all my heart and was glad of the times we had together. Go Spirit, as I shall go.' Scott turned defiantly away. With his back to this spirit he failed to see the sad aura surrounding the ghost of his fiancée, like a light blue hue immersing her body, that faded into nothingness, taking Naomi away.

The inner doors swung open, allowing the Aberdeen chilly night to creep into the Noose and Monkey Bar like an unwelcome guest at a party. Douglas shook loose his overcoat and hung it up on the hat stand before making his way to the bar.

'Fit like Douglas?' asked the barman, a broad heavily tattooed Aberdonian, more used to pulling oil pipes than pints. The oil recession had hit everyone hard, and now work was harder to find and people like Ronnie had to retrain and adapt to a new life, often with a much lower salary.

'Aye, nae bad Ronnie, nae bad,' understated Douglas who was in fact still in a bit of a state at seeing his son perform first aid on the actor. Even when someone asked a stoic Aberdeen man how he is, he would always say all was well, even if it wasn't.

'Pint o the usual is it?' enquired Ronnie.

'Aye, Ronnie, please,' replied Douglas licking his dry lips, anticipating the taste of the rejuvenating Caledonian three hops, not realising just how thirsty he was. He looked at the gleaming bar pumps with an expectant relish.

'On your own tonight, nae loon, thocht he was on leave?' Ronnie asked as he concentrated on getting the angle of the lager glass right so that a beautiful looking head would appear from the frothing liquid like a cloud on a cheery summery sky.

'Aye, the loon's right behind me, I think he went to wash his hands of the blood,' replied Douglas looking to his left and beyond the double doors.

'Blood!' replied a shocked Ronnie, the lager over spilling the pint glass and soaking down his hands and into the overspill drip tray. Those unscrupulous barmen who reused this liquid to help maintain profits referred to it as manager's skin, though this tied brewery pub had an allowance for this waste and hygienically disposed of it. 'Fit's been going on?'

'Oh, I thought you'd have heard as I was the last one out,' Douglas looked around him, seeing just how empty the bar and restaurant was, just a few diners to his left, up the few stairs, in the much sought after snug and private area. 'Oh, I thought some folks fae the theatre might have headed here.' The near empty bar and restaurant was another sign of the pulling out of the oil companies from the Las Vegas of the North East, pubs were starting to empty if not close their doors for good. Even one or two of the most loved and famous of Aberdeen hotels had been forced to close their doors due to low occupancy. More jobs were lost and property developers around the North East were rubbing their hands at their new acquisitions. 'An actor fell aff the stage at the Theatre, you should have heard the crack his bone made when he landed, puir mannie then had a heart attack,' replied Douglas as he put one foot onto the brass foot rail to help ease himself up onto the high wooden chair. He wiggled around and got comfortable.

'Geez ooh,' replied Ronnie as he dried Douglas' pint glass and then his hands with a tea towel. He looked sadly at his work and couldn't see any frothy foamy head on the lager. He shook his head and then looked over at his manager who was up the few steps, talking to a small group of diners in the wee snug area, recommending the dishes the chef had asked her to push. 'Here, have this on the house, you deserve it after seeing that.'

'Lovely, thanks Ronnie,' replied Douglas not believing his luck in getting a free drink in the Granite City. 'Though it's ma loon who deserves it really ye ken.'

'Oh fit why?' enquired Ronnie as he placed the free drink in front of a now seated Douglas.

'Well he leapt into action, ran down to the injured actor whilst we were still sat on our erses, ordered a'body about and saved the mannies life. Fit a boy!' beamed Douglas, at last parching his thirst as he took a long gulp of his pint; it tasted even sweeter as it was on the house.

'Michty me!' replied Ronnie, 'so where is he?'

'That's the odd thing, as I was leaving the paramedics were loading the puir wee mannie onto their ambulance and one minute Scott was there, just looking up at the stage as if mesmerised by a performer, and then the next minute he'd simply vanished. I hope he's alright?'

Chapter 7

Scott stumbled in his haste as he ran to flee from the spirit that he thought had

assumed his dead fiancée's identity. He righted himself by clutching onto the

banister of the stairwell, his intended destination was to get back to the main

theatre and get out of the building as fast as he could, back to the safety of his

father. He hadn't looked back; he did not want to see what fresh torments the

demon had dreamed up. If only Jake was still here, perhaps he could help fight

the spirit, the demon. 'Jake,' he croaked in desperation. He stopped midway up

the stairs and coughed to regain his voice. 'JAKE!' he shouted as he looked

around in desperation. He was not coming, would not come, but why? He said

he helped folk in his building. Scott continued on his way, knowing he was

alone, but not understanding why. He ran up the few remaining steps and then

sprinted through the laundry area, surprised not to see modern washing

machines and dryers. The washer ladies had gone and he'd assumed that with

Jake going on his merry way he would have been transported back to his own

time. He took the next staircase two steps at a time and was soon running past

the dressing rooms, all their doors were shut. Remembering the route from

earlier he burst through the stage door, expecting to see the advertising billboard

in front of him and the picturesque painted scenery of Belgium behind him.

Instead, he saw the most beautifully painted canvas with a forest scene. In the distance he could make out a rambling cottage which looked incongruous with its well-maintained garden that included a mixture of vegetable plots and flower beds fenced in as if to keep the trees out, though the gate was open. He could almost reach out, bend down and run his fingers through the grass, feel for the lower branches of the trees and pick at the petals of the flowers. To his left he expected to see wires trailing on the floor and electronic machinery. Instead he saw ropes, a maze of hemp reaching down to the floor like jungle creepers below the protective canopy of trees. Only he did not feel protected, just as his world was feeling safe and secure again, just as his confidence and zest for life had returned, so had she. He heard muted whistling as figures dressed like Jake reached and pulled for the ropes that had different coloured paint on their ends. As some rose or fell, they changed the scenery around Scott. The tumbled-down cottage and immaculate gardens had now given way to a dark, dingy forest, thick with branches that repelled the light, the forest floor full of twigs, decomposing leaves and the odd broken branch. In a daze Scott continued his journey, on automatic, as if he had to reach a preordained destination. He soon found himself further on the stage, nearer the stage lights. He could smell gas and lime and in his confusion he looked down to see several gas flames at the edges of the stage. Above each was a small cylinder being heated in front of an array of lenses. This was the limelight that was used as a crude form of stage lighting to help cast shadows and illumination to the scenery and actors. Scott looked puzzled, but surely, from what he had read; HMT had the new electrical lighting installed from its beginning? He walked further on and expected to look down and see the paramedics still working on Calum. Instead he was shocked to see an audience, a packed theatre, all dressed in their finery. Ladies wore evening dresses in an array of dazzling colours that glittered and shone like thousands of tiny stars on a clear night. Their hands and lower arms were covered in a selection of silk gloves. Some fanned themselves with brightly coloured fans, whilst others held up their delicate opera glasses, as if to look closely at Scott. The men wore black and white suits with black bow ties and waistcoats and brilliantly white shirts; many were smoking cigars, puffing out rings of tobacco smoke without a care in the world, or for their fellow patron's lungs, despite the theatre being non-smoking for years.

'Would you look at that fellow there Aileen; there right in the middle of the stage. What a great costume he's wearing!' boomed one of the men in the front row, pointing directly at Scott. His female companion was too busy laughing to reply.

Scott looked stunned, had he been transported back further in time? But why the historical inaccuracies over the lighting, he asked himself. He followed the eye-line of the theatre patron and looked behind him only to see an actor wearing a wolf's costume with large sticking out ears, grey fur and a painted face, rather than the expected furry mask. Beside him was a twenty something woman, make up over-exaggerated to make her look about ten years younger. She was dressed in a flowing red cloak that engulfed her skirt and most of her legs. It was fastened securely in a knot above her flowery blouse; she was carrying a basket covered in muslin.

'No, it cannae be?' he spoke out in disbelief. He ran down to the stage steps, glancing to see that the orchestra pit was now full of smartly dressed musicians busy with their instruments. Only now did Scott register the accompanying music that filled the theatre, the acoustics were enhanced by the shiny tulip decorated tiling in the stalls, below the red gold crested wallpaper, that caused the sound waves to bounce around the building like a ricocheting bullet in a ham Western film. All thoughts of Naomi had been put aside as it dawned on him what he was experiencing. The demon had transported him back to the opening night of His Majesty's Theatre, back to the 3rd December 1906.

He ran up the aisle, against the 1 in 34 shallow stage rake, determined to escape the malevolent grip of the demon, 'back to dad, he'd be safe then,' he thought, as the actors started to sing. He certainly wasn't going to hang around with these phantoms of the past for the four-hour performance. The patrons were clapping, the ladies hand noises were muffled with their long elegant gloves, it seemed to Scott that the men were clapping louder to compensate. He thought that it sounded as if they were clapping in tune to the step of his running feet, as if in mimicry to goad him onto his destination.

'Out of my way!' he screamed to the oblivious front of house staff blocking his exit by the double doors. Though they were only doing their diligent duty by waiting for any summoned request from an audience member or being available to help late arrivals swiftly and silently to their seats when an opportune moment in the performance allowed. They looked resplendent in their matching waistcoats and skirts, ready to attend to any patrons who summoned them with a wave of their hands. Scott stumbled through them, the visions ignorant of his touch. The wooden doors yielded to his outstretched palms as he anticipated having to push the heavy doors open. They seemed still corporeal despite their ghostly guardians. He reached the stalls staircase and bounded up them and crashed through to the foyer where he saw the familiar old fashioned wooden ticket office with glass frontage beyond the black and white chequered marble tiling flooring reminiscent of a giant chess board. As he made his way across he glimpsed an easel supporting a wooden hand painted sign proudly announcing: "Opening Night. Sweet Red Riding Hood." Later the musical play would be renamed Little Red Riding Hood and cut to reduce its time because eleven thirty at night was too late to be leaving the theatre for most weary Aberdonians with a 7am start in the morning. Beyond the sign was a row of staff ranging from a three-piece suited manager who was toying with his ornate pocket watch, more out of habit, than for checking the punctuality of his staff. In and out it went from his tiny waistcoat pocket to his large looking hands. Flick, flick, went the catch and top of the pocket watch as he habitually looked at the timepiece, though seconds had elapsed between glances. Across from him were more skirted and waist-coated young women with their hands clasped behind their backs, as if at ease on a parade ground. Next to them were several men with slicked back hair that was well cropped, they were also wearing waistcoats with ties above their black trousers. Fidgeting next to them were what seemed to Scott an endless array of boys in smart uniforms with dangling down epaulettes, like curtain edges, like those that Colonel Gaddafi, the Libyan dictator favoured before his overdue and inevitable downfall finally came. In these broad shouldered epaulettes the youngsters had smartly placed their gloves tightly in position, thumbs and fingers pointing downwards as if pointing to the tiles to show off how clean and gleaming they were. Each member of the staff then promptly stood smartly to attention at the nod from the theatre manager who had finally stopped flicking open his pocket watch and rested it in his waistcoat pocket for the final time that night. All eyes were nervously looking at the manager as if for commands. 'Stop moving!' he hissed across to the twitching boys to stop their constant and distracting movements.

Scott didn't hang around, not even to admire the solid looking bust in the corner which was of the architect of this fine building, Frank Matcham. It looked like time had jumped again and he was witnessing the opening night end of the show staff formation to guide their patrons out and wish them a good night. He was not sure why the demon had chosen to show him this, but he was moving fast again, straight through the open solid oak door with glass inlays.

He jumped down the two steps and found himself entering the chill of the wintery Aberdeen night. He bumped straight into an unimpressed bright red tail coated gentleman with a chubby face, made all the fatter as it was pushed up by the tight collar. Or rather he fell through this new ghost who moved his white gloved hand to his black and white peaked cap and tipped it in Scott's direction. There was a rustle of movement as if a gentleman in a noisy private club library was protesting against conversation by ruffling his broadsheet newspaper.

'Pardon me sir,' he said apologetically.

'You can see me?' enquired an incredulous Scott, staring at the man he knew to be the Rustler, the first doorman of HMT who was so nicknamed for stuffing newspapers in his trousers to help keep out the chill of the Granite City. As he moved, his big shiny coat buttons twinkled off the moon as if toying with Scott's eyes.

'Of course sir. Not all is as it seems sir. Did you enjoy the show?' he enquired of Scott as he replaced his hat and stood rigidly to attention.

'Which one?' replied Scott playfully. 'I've seen two on stage and twa unfold afore ma very eyes.'

'Very good sir, very good. She said you had a sharp wit.'

Scott stood still now, shocked and worried that the tone of conversation had taken a more sinister direction. 'She?' he asked hesitantly, fearful of the answer.

'Why Naomi, of course Scott. It really was her you know,' replied the Rustler with a twinkle in his eyes and a kind smile on his lips, 'You didn't think she'd leave you, did you. Her love for you was too strong and she…'

'NO!' interrupted Scott angrily as he reached out and tried to push the doorman from him, only remembering as he stumbled that he could not touch these phantoms, only talk and listen. As he landed in a semi-crouch on the pavement he looked across the street to see the familiar William Wallace statue, its left arm outstretched as if pointing back into the theatre, advising Scott to go back to Naomi. His right arm held proudly onto his sword. Scott ignored the inanimate statue and righted himself, just in time to jump back from a horse and carriage, the black steed dark in the dimly lit street with its gas lighting atop old fashioned lamp posts. Its clip clopping came to a resounding halt in the old cobbled street. One of the boys with the tasselled epaulettes jumped down from the rear of the carriage and raced to the foyer entrance. The Rustler, Scott all forgotten as his duty called, deftly opened the door to the ornately painted carriage to allow a smartly dressed couple to enter. She was covered in furs and he was dressed in black overcoat as protection and comfort from the harsh weather, his top hat and shiny topped stick an ornamentation of his wealth. This movement forward from the foyer to the carriage was a carefully practiced manoeuvre by the Rustler, honed with much practice so that his patrons would not get too cold or wet. He quickly pocketed his penny for his trouble from the gentleman and he shut the carriage door and ensured it was securely latched before making his way back to the Foyer to escort more VIP guests who had retrieved their hats and coats from the cloakroom attendant.

Meanwhile the carriage boy held out his hand discretely for the next gentleman to place a shiny farthing bearing King Edward VII's face looking right onto his eager hand. It disappeared swiftly, as did the boy as soon as he had received his reward, like a thief in the night. He ran up Rosemount Viaduct, alongside a carriage heading towards the affluent part of Rosemount at the top of the hill. He cheekily glanced over his shoulder to check that Harry Adair Nelson, the Theatre manager, was not looking, and then jumped onto the tailboard for a quicker ride out to bring another empty carriage and driver for more patrons. The faster he and his fellow carriage boys could bring the carriages to the departing patrons, the more tips they would secure. Though, the Lord above help any of the carriage boys who got caught doing this strictly forbidden practice that could result in injury or death: Nelson's wrath could be severe. His reputation, even on this opening night, was one of an ardent follower of rules and as a strict disciplinarian to those who did not follow his word and commands.

Scott looked on with fascination. He had never been privy to so many phantoms at one time. Was this Naomi's work because she knew he loved history and his beloved Aberdeen, especially this Theatre? They had spent many a night at HMT enjoying pantomimes and plays over the years during their leave from military duties. They had even joined the Friends of Aberdeen Performing Arts scheme so that they could get discounted tickets and attend special events such as when they met the cast of An Inspector Calls. No, he thought, she was dead and not here, whatever that was, that manifestation, it was not his lover. He shook his head in an effort to clear it. William Wallace was still pointing towards the area known as Transportation, Damnation,

Salvation and Education by generations of Aberdeen folk. Transportation because of the old and long gone Schoolhill Railway Station that was convenient for the delivery of hand painted large scenery canvases. Damnation because of the debauchery that was said to go on in Victorian and Edwardian theatres when actresses were often common prostitutes. Salvation for the building next door that was the soul saving South United Church and that now was St Mark's. And lastly education for the public library that stood at the end of this row. Across from this was the actor's haven, the Well o' Spa Bar, which sadly closed decades ago and is now the site of the Denburn Health Centre. 'Hospitalisation or ministration!' thought Scott wryly, trying to get his befuddled brain to add to the weel-kent, the well-known rhyme. During this the Kemnay and Tillyfourie quarried granite twinkled away in the moonlight as if acting as aircraft guiding lights for Scott to get closer towards his father. As if remembering his destination, he turned and made his way determinedly to the Noose and Monkey, moving past the throng of opening night patrons making their way home under the watchful eye of Chief Constable Anderson and his Constables. They had been drafted in to ensure that everything went safely and under control. Scott had had enough of these theatre ghosts, the Honorary Chaplain from the Actor's Church Union could sort them out if people still saw them, he thought. As Scott made his way through them he looked up at the central parapet at the front entrance to see the statue of Tragedy and Comedy by Mr Arrowsmith, created to match those inside His Majesty's Theatre. Unlike

William Wallace, the sword of tragedy was well gone, lost to the elements. This indicated to Scott that time was advancing, since the sword was only lost in the last few decades. Before his eyes the theatre was lit proudly with modern electric blue lights that reflected down to give a green glowing effect. The blue gas lampposts were still there, but now had electric lighting. He walked past Donald's Way as he made it to the railings of St Mark's Church and looked up to see the familiar smaller green hued dome, like a baby version of the HMT dome. He could hear the familiar peep peep of the Pelican crossing taking walkers to Union Terrace and was soon by the ornate low pillars of the Central Library that supported this tall Gothic-looking building that housed rows of cooing pigeons on its roof, plumped down against the elements, settling down to sleep in the dim glow of the moon. They did not hear the familiar 'Rubidub dum' that seemed to grow louder in Scott's head as if marching him in step towards his father. He ignored the feathered iron blue lamps of the library steps and continued on his way past the granite dome which was in sharp contrast to the two green coppered domes. He crossed the road, no longer used by horse and carriage, but now smooth and used by modern day cars that beeped at him for daring to cross without waiting for the green man to guide him safely across.

He'd made it; he'd reached the cleverly curved granite four storied building that housed the Noose and Monkey on the corner of Skene Street and Rosemount Viaduct. He just had to squeeze through the ubiquitous smokers that seemed to hang around under a fog of cigarette smoke at every pub in

Scotland's doorways since the smoking ban. The large old fashioned pyramidal lamp above the outer doorway lighted the emberic glows of their cigarettes. As Scott stumbled through the inner doors and into the bar he sought out his father and reached out and embraced him.

'Alright son,' he said returning the unexpected, but welcome embrace, worried upon seeing the distress in Scott's face before he buried it in his father's shoulder, 'you look like you need a dram o whisky!'

'Nae, faither, I've had enough spirits tonight,' replied Scott to his frowning father.

Chapter 8

Douglas stood back from the warm embrace having enjoyed feeling physically close to his son, happy to relish the paternal intimacy. He was glad that Scott was back, and immensely proud of his son. He held onto Scott's shoulders as he withdrew, 'Are you alright son?' he enquired with deep concern in his voice. 'Did you mean that you've already had a drink? I was only speaking figuratively; I ken you're not allowed to drink with the pills you are on. Did someone at the Theatre give you a calming dram?'

'Sorry dad, I was just thinking out loud, I wish I could have a drink after the night I've just had,' replied Scott, hoping to put his father's mind at rest.

'Is the loon alright, that actor fellow?' enquired Douglas, of Calum. 'I was really proud of how you helped him and saw he was alright. I've never seen you perform your army and nursing training: you did really well Scott. Your mother would have been that proud of you son, I know I am. You were just as bossy as she was!'

'Och, aye, he'll be fine,' replied Scott, seeing the tears start to build up in the eyes of his emotional father, despite his attempt at humour. 'The paramedics looked like they kent fit to do,' he quickly continued to help calm his dad down. 'He'd have been taken to the A&E department at Aberdeen Royal Infirmary quicker than you can down a pint!'

Douglas took the hint and offered, 'Hear, let me get you a drink, the usual fizzy apple with ice is it?' asked Douglas as he let go of Scott's shoulders and stepped back to take in his son, to make sure he was really alright. Looking down at Scott's hands he blurted out, 'Michty me min, I thocht you were going to wash your hands. Look at the state of ye ma loon, you're a clarty with blood. Get yerself tae the toilets and have a good wash loon, whilst I get a couple of menus and your well-deserved drink. I'll get your favourite table by the window so you can golk oot at a'body passing by when my conversation gets too boring for you,' ordered Douglas like a dad to a young child, feeling protective towards his adult son.

Scott looked down at his hands and as he turned them over, events from the past flashed swiftly and fleetingly before his eyes, times when his hands had been thick with the blood of colleagues in combat. Wounded and dying men's and women's faces came back to haunt him in an instant, men and women who, despite his best efforts, he could not save in foreign lands, serving their country, far from loved ones. It was always the guilt that started the tears, the guilt of not being able to save someone's son, brother, father, daughter, sister, wife or husband. Or his beloved Naomi. Seeing the look of concern in his father's face he quickly snapped out of his morbid reverie and turned his palms upwards, they were dull red and crusted; blotches of darkened red were on his top and trousers and had even stained his new trainers to a dull ochre patchwork.

'Aye, I'll not be long; I'll go and scrub up. A fizzy apple will be great, thanks Dad.' With that he walked across to the gent's toilet, passing the kitchen door from which appetising smells were wafting out, tickling and arousing his stomach, causing it to growl loud with hunger like a lion finally spotting its vulnerable prey's weakness after a long hunt. At times Scott wondered if he had become detached and immune to the bodily trauma of others because rather than dulling his appetite, performing emergency first aid out in the field, or within hospitals, always made him so hungry afterwards. With others it usually suppressed their appetite, lunches and dinners went untouched, cigarettes and alcohol helped some though. He silently hoped he was not becoming immune to the suffering of others as he had always prided himself on his caring, sympathetic nature. He swung open the bathroom door, turned the tight corner, ignored the urinals and made for the first sink.

"Rubidub dum, rubidub dum" went the noises in his head, getting louder and louder. Despite trying to ignore them, Scott screwed up his face. He knew they were getting louder and more intrusive and that he must talk to his Counsellor or Community Psychiatric Nurse about them. But would they understand, how could he even begin to talk to someone about what he had been experiencing since his encounter with the Grey Lady?

Looking over his shoulder he could see the toilet cubicle door was closed. He did not want an audience to overhear his usual coping mechanism of shouting 'GET OUT OF MY HEAD!' when he was alone, so he concentrated on washing his hands. As he turned on the tap and wetted his hands under the water he thought back to the first week of nurse training many years ago. He and his fellow student nurses had been asked to put a harmless liquid onto their hands by their tutor. Then they were told to go and wash their hands thoroughly. When they came back the tutor had turned off the lights and shone an ultra violet light over their palms, backs of hands, fingers and thumbs. The areas that were still blue were places not thoroughly washed and were contaminated. They all learnt a valuable lesson on the importance of hand hygiene that day and were taught the correct procedure of hand washing, something Scott continued in his professional and private life since.

Yet it wasn't enough to take his mind off the noises as they grew louder with each beat, "rubidub dum, rubidub dum," they continued as Scott reached out to the automatic soap dispenser on the wall. He was mildly annoyed to find it empty, but impressed when he looked to the far left sink, by the cubicle, to find that the thoughtful staff of the Noose and Monkey had placed a blue and white pump-action container of liquid soap there. He moved across to get it and noticed that the cubicle must have been empty all along as under the gap he could see no feet. He pumped out a generous helping of the sea kelp scented soap and lathered away as he was taught, palm to palm. He then placed his right hand over the left palm and interlaced his fingers, all the time working the soap deeply into his hands and fingers ensuring he interlocked his fingers and rubbed the back of them. He then rotated his left thumb through his right palm whilst moving to clasp it, all the time the light blue coloured soap began turning pink and then crimson as the remnants of Calum's dried blood seeped down the plughole. Scott repeated the procedure in reverse for his other hand, fingers and thumb. He breathed in deeply and was pleased to smell the salty tangy cleansing smell of the seaweed soap, rather than the cloying coppery overpowering smell of stale blood. He rinsed himself thoroughly with the warming water and pumped out more soap and repeated the procedure; wanting to rid himself of all of Calum's blood, glad that his Hepatitis vaccinations were up to date. As he watched the fading scarlet soapy suds disappear down the sink he turned off the taps.

The "rubidub dum, rubidub dum," noises were getting louder and more frantic sounding as they echoed around the porcelain urinals and tiles on the walls. In this enclosed room they sounded as if they were reaching into Scott's soul and trying to take hold deep within him. As Scott reached out to the Dyson hand dryer he caught sight of himself in the mirror. Streaks of blood were smeared across his face as if a chef was decorating a plate for fancy dining with beetroot sauce. Worst of all was his dishevelled hair and frightened rabbit in headlamp eyes. As he returned to the sink to wash his face he tried simultaneously to perform his deep breathing exercises and go to his special relaxing place in his mind. "Rubidub dum, rubidub dum," beat with every splash onto his face until he could take it no longer, 'STOP!' he shouted above the din of the pop singer blaring out from the bar and restaurant speakers that penetrated as a distant boom into the bathroom and helped to mask his fervent screaming to the outside world. 'PLEASE. JUST. STOP.'

The "rubidub dum, rubidub dum," got louder and louder, accompanied by rhythmic banging that filled the spaces between beats. It sounded now like an orchestra was in full inharmonious flow without the fervent thrusting and pulling guiding baton of a mad looking jerking, convulsing conductor. Each instrument was just bashing out their own tune for all they were worth. Scott thumped the tiles above the sink in frustration and in the mirror looked to the cubicle, the source of the noise. He turned around smartly and took a few steps nearer to it.

'Is anyone in there?' he shouted through the door, following through his question with a sharp knock on the door. It yielded slightly to his touch. It was unlocked.

There was no reply; just the regular bang, bang noises. The "rubidub dum, rubidub dum," was slowly fading to a residual echo. In contrast, the bangs were getting louder and louder, until Scott, in frustration, flung open the cubicle door, oblivious to anyone's modesty, his need to quieten the noises was more urgent than offending their humility. If there was an occupant sitting down, performing a natural act, he'd get an unwelcome guest. Still, nothing he hadn't seen before on the wards.

It was empty, just the usual scraps of fallen loo roll were on the floor, escaping wetness that was gathering around the toilet seat floor. Scott spotted the open window that was moving with the wind of the wild Aberdeen night like a boxer against a well-worn punch bag, relentlessly tap tapping away. With each opening and closing more dreich Aberdeen rain was getting in and running down the wall to the floor. The latch was broken; it was missing from the window frame. Instead someone had used a cable tie in an attempt to close the window against the bar frames. This was the cause of the banging; it hadn't been tied tight enough. As if in confirmation it continued to beat against the wooden framework with each gust of wind. The frosted over glass vibrated with each thud adding to the cacophony of noise, like an inopportune percussionist. Scott exhaled deeply and returned to the dryer and as he sunk his hands into the welcome warm air he felt relief that he was not going mad and imagining these noises. Though his doubt lurked at the back of his mind like a niggling toothache that resurfaces to the bite of sugar as a reminder of its presence and the need for treatment. But what of the other noises? He could not explain those that he heard over the last few months.

He sighed deeply again and made his way out of the bathroom. As he entered the main bar he caught sight of the familiar shape of his dad's back leaning against a chair, now seated at a table, looking out of the window at the passing traffic and pedestrians. Scott made his way to the table. As he drew nearer he was able to make out more of the table and the seat in front of his dad, on the other side, facing the bar. There, sat down and leaning forward, chin clasped restfully in her hands, as if staring fondly into his dad's eyes, as if in deep rapturous conversation, was his beloved Naomi.

Chapter 9

Could this be her; could this really be Naomi come back to him? What if this wasn't a demon or shapeshifter or whatever? After all, the Grey Lady was able to stay decades at the Cambridge Military Hospital after her death. She even nursed patients from beyond the grave. But surely he had taken over her special role, after all, he could talk with the ghosts, help them find their peace. All these thoughts went whizzing around Scott's head as he walked, albeit more slowly and hesitantly now, to his father. Could Dad see her? Is that what he was looking mesmerised at?

Sensing his approach Douglas stood up, not through some paternal sixth sense, but more prosaically because he'd heard the bathroom door spring back closed with a dull thump. 'Would you look at that daft feel loon over there, a night like this and no jacket on, just a flimsy t-shirt to show off his puny guns. You should go after him and show him your muscles Scott, that'll encourage him to cover up!'

Scott laughed, more to cover up his shock at seeing Naomi again, and with his dad, rather than being amused at his joke. 'Aye, and I get my gym for free, I bet he pays a fortune to work out!'

Douglas grinned, glad to hear Scott joke again and looking clean, though his clothes still bore blood. If only Rhona was still with him, she'd know how to get rid of the blood from her son's clothes. He'd only just got the hang of the washing machine and all the different cycles, buttons and flashing lights 'Och well,' he said aloud as he turned to move to the other chair. 'You come and sit down here and have a turn at watching the world go by son.'

'Naw. You're alright where you are Dad, I fancy sitting over there the nicht, you sit yourself back doon,' Scott replied. He didn't just want not to trouble his dad who looked comfortable. He had noticed Naomi look up and smile her beautiful radiant beam at him. God, she was gorgeous he thought. As if sensing his thoughts, she then indicated that he should sit down next to her by patting the adjacent seat enthusiastically. Well, he thought morosely, let's see what happens when I sit on you. With that thought still in his head he shuffled around the table and effortlessly eased back the chair and promptly sat down. Nothing. He'd expected Naomi, or whatever it was, to manifest through him in a puff of smoke, like in the films. Perhaps even for an arm to reach through his chest, but again nothing. Out of the corner of his eye he could see that she was sitting next to him in the vacant chair, smiling serenely. Since when did she start smiling serenely, thought Scott? She was always so tomboyish and loud; definitely not serene. Death must have mellowed her, he thought. No, it's not her, it's another ghost, but she does look...

Scott's dad interrupted his thoughts. 'I don't know why I get you a menu; you always have the same thing here. Let me guess; haggis bon-bons for starters and beef olives for the main. Am I right or what?'

85

'Aye,' replied Scott, glad of the interruption, 'you ken me well. I cannae resist deep fried haggis. I love the crunchy batter and then the soft spicy meatiness of the haggis. And the beef olives are always wrapped around oatmeal, rather than sausage meat like in other places. They have a proper Scot's chef here, affa talented. He's able to get the silverside steak to cook perfectly too, not too tough and not raw. Not as good as mum's though, she was a great cook. I'm surprised we weren't a couple of fatties when she was alive. Especially you, with the big box of treats she'd pack for your work.'

'Aye, she was a lovely mother to you and wife tae me. I really miss her, and so do the boys at work. The secret, which I think she knew, was that I always shared out the cakes and goodies to the other loons and quines in the office, they especially loved her black bun, they couldn't get enough of it and eagerly waited for each New Year when they kent I'd be in with a big cake tin of it.

'Ha ha, aye, she knew right enough, that's why she always made twa or three of them. She telt me and asked me not to let on. I used to help her when I was younger.' Scott's eyes misted up at the thought of the other great loss in his life. He looked to his side, straight into the eyes of Naomi and sighed deeply before turning back to his dad.

'Aye, Hogmanay is not the same without her or her black bun, a'body in the office still talk about her and her affa fine pastry crust and rich fruit cake. I tried making one a few years back, but it was a disaster, even the garden birds flew away when I put it out on the bird table. I buy one from Thain's Bakery in

86

George Street now and take it in when I'm on shift in the New Year, but it's not the same. Tasty mind, but not the same, she had a special touch in the kitchen your mither.' Now it was Douglas' turn to sigh, both united in their grief. 'I still see her you know.'

'What, mum?' asked an incredulous Scott. Did they share a common ability to see their loved ones after death? Could he share his sightings of Naomi with his father?

'Aye, but I ken it's nae her. It was worse at the beginning. Everywhere I went there would always be someone who looked like her. That's what I mean. Maybe in a hairstyle, the way someone walked or even the same type of clothes. It was the same when poor Bess had to be put down. When she was alive you wouldn't see another Flat-Coated Retriever, yet after she'd gone it seemed like every other dog in the park was a flattie, bless her.'

'Ah miss them both, mum more, lots more.'

Douglas reached across to hold his son's hand. He knew he was talking about Naomi and not Bess when he said both. He knew how much he missed his mum and no amount of overcompensating could overcome that. God knows how Scott coped after Naomi's shocking death. Though he knew that he didn't cope, no amount of paternal hugs could help his son.

'Aye, two grand lassies. I wish they could be here now,' sighed Douglas.

Scott watched Naomi stand up and walk around the table. She put her arms around Douglas and appeared to kiss him on the cheek. It looked like she was truly cuddling him. No part of her spiritual body was flowing through him but there was a soft orange glow given off, as if Naomi was transferring her love to his dad. Could this truly be Naomi, he thought?

His dad interrupted his thoughts once more, 'If I had her here now I'd tell her how much I loved her and miss her. I'd consider myself the luckiest man in the world to have even one more second with your mum.' Douglas shivered, though they were sat next to a radiator and it was cosy warm inside the restaurant and bar. 'Anyway,' he said, lifting up his almost empty pint towards Scott. 'Cheers loon!'

Scott picked up his drink and clinked glasses with his dad, 'Aye Faither, cheers! You're a guid man, always talking sense to me. While his dad finished off his drink Scott turned to Naomi who had returned to her seat after the cuddle.

'I love you Scott,' she said 'it really is me.'

'Aye, I ken lass, I ken,' muttered Scott, waking up to his good fortune but not wanting to talk to Naomi in public in case his father thought him insane and rushed him up to Royal Cornhill, the psychiatric hospital two streets away. He, at last, smiled lovingly back to her.

'Fit's that loon?' asked Douglas pointing to the big screen on the far wall. That wifie on the telly is an affa loud singer.'

Scott laughed; sudden joy in his voice, he was glad he'd not been heard. He looked across to the TV on the centre of the stag and thistle wallpapered wall, but gratefully all he saw was his beloved Naomi, miraculously back from the dead, wondrously by his side. 'I said I'm ready dad, I don't need to look, I know what I want.'

Douglas looked pleased, he was very hungry, even though they'd eaten earlier at the 1906 restaurant; he was looking forward to his Balmoral chicken and another pint. He wondered if Ronnie might sneak him another crafty freebie. Aye, an Aberdonian pigs might fly and ghosts may appear he thought wryly.

Chapter 10

Julie, the manager of the Noose and Monkey, walked over to Scott and Douglas, her ponytail bouncing playfully against her shoulders with each step. She'd discretely left them alone, having been informed earlier by Ronnie what they'd both seen and done at the Theatre. As she reached their table she gave Scott his customary naughty wink, alerting him that mischief was afoot. 'Okay lads, I'm going to need your order, chef knocks off in ten minutes and he's a moody bugger at the best of times. The usual is it Scott?'

'Aye, please Julie, though maybe just the main tonight,' said Scott taking out his iPhone from his pocket to check the time. 'I didnae realise it was so late. Dad's on an early shift tomorrow. We weren't expecting to be out so late.'

'Aye, aye, a couple o lads oot on the toon, watch oot the quines of Aberdeen! And what are you having handsome?' asked Julie turning to Douglas who gave his habitual blush at her usual question.

'Er, aye, just a Balmoral chicken for me please lass,' he replied, clearly embarrassed.

Julie tapped away on her hand-held device which wirelessly sent their request to the chef. She was relieved that he would be alone to hear the click and whirr of the printout in the kitchen as two more meals were ordered just before his shift ended at ten o'clock. That'll teach the temperamental sweary old bugger, she thought. Serves him right! She didn't fancy having to listen to more of his ranting complaints. Mind you, it was worth putting up with because his food was fantastic and they were always packed out at the weekends.

Scott's dad looked at the device in Julie's hand, still in awe that their order could be sent so quickly, no matter how often he'd sat and watched her click away on its screen. He'd often compared it to the Star Trek communicator to Scott, original series of course! He'd loved the engineer character so much that he managed to convince Rhona that Scott would make a lovely name for their son, though she soon put a stop to him calling him Scotty.

'These are on the house, you two, it was really good what you did for that actor tonight,' said Julie to Scott, reaching over to pat him on the shoulder fondly. Douglas near choked on his pint as he was trying to finish it and involuntary spat some back into the glass. 'You alright there handsome, do you need a refill?'

'Oh, aye, yes please lass, the usual,' replied Douglas between coughs.

'Okay, dokay, lover boy, I'll be back in a minute or two. Don't be missing me now!' she laughed as she walked away.

'I do love it when Julie is on duty, she really winds you up, doesn't she handsome!' Scott blew a kiss to his father.

'Dinnae you start, I get enough ribbing fae the lads at work after that time we had a staff night out here and she was all over me. Imagine a quine of that age fawning over a silly auld bugger like me.'

91

'Och, ye ken she's only messing about with you, a bit of harmless flirting. She only does it to you because she knows you're too much of a gentleman to reciprocate. If she did that to any of the other regulars, then she'd have eager hands all over her in places she disnae want them. But you do go a lovely shade of red though Dad!'

'Aye, well, I never was much good with the lassies; I was even shy with your mum.'

'Whooa, spare the details, there are some things a son should not hear from his faither. So, when I'm away, do you not go out with any special lass?'

'No,' replied Douglas sounding more serious now. 'I could never love another after your mum, she was very special.'

'Aye, she was, a lovely mother too, so she was,' reminisced Scott. 'I feel the same way about Naomi, I could never love another after the wonderful relationship we had.' Scott felt a warm glow at his side and looked to see Naomi was cuddling up to him, he looked quickly away so as not to make his father wonder what he was looking at. He had a broad smile on his face and was so bursting with happiness and couldn't wait to get Naomi on her own and find out why she was able to return to him. He was convinced that it was definitely her.

'But it's different for you Scott. I know how much you loved that sweet lass, but you're young enough to find someone special again and fall in love. What about that ambulance lassie, what was her name?'

'Yvonne?'

'Aye, see, she let you know her name straight away, I saw the way she looked at you, eyes meeting across a crowded stage and all that.'

'Away min, that was just professional courtesy,' replied Scott, trying desperately hard not to look to Naomi. He knew she'd be punching his arm at this. Which led him on another train of thought, would she always be with him, why was she back and could they have a physical relationship once more? 'Besides,' he said to his dad, 'it was a crowded orchestra pit.'

'Here we are gorgeous, here's your knife and fork,' said Julie putting down a napkin and cutlery by Douglas and then Scott, 'your meal is just being lovingly prepared by chef just now. Winnae be lang.'

'Cheers Julie,' said Scott, hoping to save his dad more embarrassing blushes by keeping her distracted. 'Tell me something. I've been coming here for years and never thought to ask, why's the bar called The Noose and Monkey anyway?'

'It was the previous owners; they didn't like the old name. You probably don't mind it, being so young, but handsome here,' she continued as she gave Douglas a quick and sly cuddle, 'will remember it as The Silver Slipper'.

'Away aff me quine, I'm auld enough to ken it as My Father's Moustache, a daft name if you ask me. Mind you, you're daft enough to like that name! An get aff me, I'm auld enough to be your faither,' joked Douglas giving Julie a taste of her own medicine, flapping his hands around his body as if maintaining his personal space.

She let off a riotous laugh that carried across to the other diners in the snug area and caused Ronnie to pause in polishing glasses and look over. 'Naughty, naughty Douglas!' she replied whilst winking at Scott. 'They came up from Hartlepool to run the pub and were enamoured with the tale that their fishermen told about a French warship that floundered off the coast, way back when the Duke of Wellington, now that's a right proper pub name, was at war with Napoleon…'

Scott sat upright, he loved military history and interrupted Julie's flow, 'During the Napoleonic Wars Dad, like in that documentary we watched the other night, well I watched, you were snoring your head off.'

'Well as I was saying,' she nudged Douglas, 'are you awake for this sleepy head?' she joked to him, giving Scott another cheeky wink. 'Anyway when the locals went to the ship, hoping for some plunder and spoils of war, you'll never guess what they found?'

'Gold?' asked Douglas hopefully.

'Naw, dozey, only a blooming monkey dressed up in a French naval uniform complete with bicorn hat.'

'Away lass!' replied Douglas in astonishment.

'No, really, it was tied to the wheel. There were no humans aboard, just the monkey. The locals, having never seen a Frenchman before, thought this was one. So they tried it and sentenced it to hang, they thought it was a spy, and hang it they did, just like that monkey in Boddam by Peterhead that was hung by the locals.'

'Oh, wait a minute,' said Douglas, warming to the tale, 'that'll be why Hartlepool Football Club are called the Monkey Hangers then. It's a fitting nickname and they've even a mascot called H'Angus, the H must be for hanged. Mind you, the first fan to don the costume did some naughty things on the pitch, the cheeky monkey.'

'Och, you men, it's always football with you lot, bad enough that I have to watch it and see you all making fools of yourself when it's on that big screen,' replied Julie, ignoring the bad pun. They all looked across to the television which was now showing the news; Scott took the opportunity to smile at Naomi whilst they were occupied. Oh God please let it be her, I pray you'll let her stay with me, thought Scott surprising himself that since his mother's death he'd given a small but hopeful, passionate prayer.

'No really, they've even a monkey mascot,' replied Douglas now on a more comfortable subject matter since he always felt under-knowledgeable with Scott over military history. At least now he could shine though he couldn't resist asking, 'So why did the folk fae Boddam hang their monkey? Was it dressed as Napoleon?'

'No, this tale is slightly different. They wanted to claim salvage rights to a stricken vessel on their rocks and could only do so if there were no survivors. But they found a live monkey; it was probably being kept as a pet by one of the drowned sailors back from exotic lands. Anyway the Boddam folk hung it in their greed. That's why the old song is called The Boddamers hung the Monkey-O.'

'Give us a wee turn of the song then lass,' asked Douglas as a bell was tinkled.

'Saved by the bell Douglas, that'll be Mr Grumpy announcing your meals are ready. I'll be back in a minute, don't be yearning for me while I'm gone handsome!' said Julie, letting her fingers glide gently across Douglas' shoulders, like a dove spreading its wings and using the gentle wind to come into land to its dovecote.

'You know,' said Scott conspiratorially once Julie was out of earshot, 'I'm not so sure that she is joking, I think she really fancies you.'

'Awa min,' replied Douglas, sitting up straighter in his chair and puffing out his chest, 'do you really think so?'

'Aye, some lassies like the aulder man,' continued Scott to his father, who was unaware that he was winding him up and getting him on the hook, ready to reel in. Naomi, still sat by Scott's side, gave him a playful thump on the arm, which, unseen by him, did go through him this time, and was not even felt by him. 'Why don't you ask her out when she comes back,' finished Scott.

'Naw, dinnae be daft,' replied Douglas, but with doubt in his mind.

'Well, here's your chance, here she comes with our dinner.'

'Here we are, my two favourite customers, beef olives for you Scott, and Balmoral chicken for you Douglas,' said Julie delicately putting their meals down in front of them. She was puzzled at the open-mouthed expression on the face of Douglas. 'Is everything alright sweetheart?'

'Aye, love, can I ask you something?'

'Of course lover boy, ask away, but nothing too naughty now!'

'D, d, do you have any salt please lass?' stammered Douglas.

Chapter 11

'Don't be so cruel to your dad Scott, you naughty boy!' whispered Naomi, almost seductively, close to Scott's right ear.

He was surprised to feel a light breeze, like a small wind playing gently with a dandelion head. Could ghosts get seductive thought Scott, could they breathe air out? He laughed, not just at his dad's discomfort, but also because he was wondering why Naomi was bothering to whisper when clearly no-one could see or hear her. Otherwise his dad wouldn't have been able to contain himself; he missed her almost as much as Scott had done. Though would dad have kept as calm as Scott thought he himself had done, especially if he'd seen as many ghosts as he had tonight, especially at the decapitation?

'Well, I'm glad you found that funny ma loon, go on, have a good laugh, get it out of your system, why don't you,' said Douglas, feigning indignation and pulling a sulking face.

'Sorry faither,' replied Scott, who evidently was anything but sorry. 'For a moment there I really thought you were going to ask her out on a hot date. I'd have loved to have known if she'd have said yes or no.' He looked over to his dad who was cutting open his chicken, through the thick creamy whisky flavoured sauce, to get to the steaming haggis within.

Douglas daubed some of the moist haggis onto his boiled new baby potatoes and prepared his fork, ready to enjoy his second meal of the day, but not before saying to Scott, 'You almost had me believing you, ye daftie! Then I caught sight of myself and my grey hair and wrinkly face in the window reflection and recovered just in time. I'm well over auld for that lassie.'

'Aye, I ken, since faun have you ever taken salt tae your food, good recovery though, I'll give you that. Who knew my dad was such a quick thinker? Besides, I think your grey hair makes you look distinguished, like George Clooney.'

Naomi got up and moved across to sit in the seat next to Douglas, a physical demonstration of her support for Douglas and her disapproval of Scott, though she too was still laughing, despite waggling her finger in displeasure at Scott, who continued to smile.

'Well, it was worth it to see the smile back on your face loon. You deserve to be happy again,' said Douglas as he tucked into more of his food.

'I ken we only ate at the 1906 Restaurant four hours ago, but I'm starving, I knew I should have had lunch,' said Scott as he cut into the beef olives and was soon engulfed with the steamy aromas of oatmeal.'

'I'm just glad to see you eating again, and having your appetite back. All those months of visiting you at Birmingham and then Headley Court made me sick with worry. You carried your grief around like a giant tortoise shell stuck on your back, weighing you down. I didn't like having to leave you and come back to work, but I needed the job to pay for the house so you'd have somewhere tae bide. But stubbornly you went and bought that lovely flat in Aldershot and wanted to live on your own. I truly thought the army would have forced you to leave.'

Scott subconsciously fingered the scar at his throat, proof of just how ill he had been. He'd had to have a tracheostomy fitted in Afghanistan. 'Aye, my Matron and Commanding Officer really did fight my corner dad.'

'Aye, and that lovely Padre, nae bad for a Yorkshireman,' replied Douglas, unaware that Naomi had perked up at the mention of Padre Caldwell. She smiled across to Scott. He returned the gesture, knowing that she'd love to see him again. Now that she was sat across from him he could pretend to be looking at the bar and meet her gaze without his father thinking he was odd. How lovely life was becoming he thought. How beautiful she looked; it truly was her, wasn't it?

'Anyway, after this leave what are you up too?' enquired Douglas of his son.

Scott pointed to his mouth, indicating he was chewing, something he always did when waiters came across asking how the food was, just as he'd taken a big bite. He'd usually just give them a big thumbs-up gesture and continue chewing, rather than speak with a mouth full of food.

His mum had brought him up well, thought Douglas of his well-mannered son. They both had.

'Never mind changing the subject,' warned Scott once his mouth was empty of his mashed tatties. 'When are you going to go on a date with a nice lady, mum wouldn't have wanted you to be lonely all this time?' nagged Scott.

'I'm not lonely son; I've ma pigeons at hame and I get oot and aboot an affa lot. Not as often as when Naomi was with us, the race meetings aren't the same without her. But the lads and quines at work are great company and we go on lots of work nights out. Otherwise staring at the traffic control screens all day long would drive us barmy. You see, I just keep the buses of Aberdeen ticking along all day and night, but you have a much more important job son. I saw that tonight; you really make a difference.'

'Och,' replied Scott, who now took his turn to be embarrassed and red-faced, clearly an inherited trait. 'Nae really, it all seems so dull after Iraq, The Stan, Sierra Leone and Nepal.'

'Well I'm glad you are away from those places, I'm glad you've got all your limbs...'

'But not my sanity,' interrupted Scott looking directly at Naomi, shadows of doubt danced in his head whilst he briefly wondered if his Post Traumatic Stress Disorder or recovering head injury was the cause of her manifestation. He really hoped not.

'But you're on the mend again, aren't you,' replied Douglas worriedly.

'Please don't worry about me, dad, I've completed all my treatments and have been given the all clear. I just need to take my pills and carry on certain mindfulness exercises. Thanks for coming with me to the first few classes; it really did make the difference with my confidence.'

'Nae bither son, always glad to help.' It really was no bother for Douglas as he continued to reveal; 'I learnt a few handy things about myself at them.'

Naomi reached over to cuddle Douglas again, as if thanking him for looking after Scott. Both men ate in companionable silence, relishing their late meal and each other's company.

As Douglas rubbed his mouth free of the last of the whisky sauce with his napkin, he again asked Scott what he would be doing for work next.

Scott became animated, as he always did about his job to his dad. 'It's really exciting, well I think it is. The army boffins have developed a new painkiller for out in the field. It's based on the strong painkiller Fentanyl. It's 100 times more effective than Morphine and the cleverest thing is that it can be given as a lollipop.'

'Fit! A lollipop?' asked a dubious Douglas.

'No really! In combat we are being trained to tape it to the finger of a casualty and then we get them to rub it against their gums, around the mouth, teeth and cheek. It gets absorbed through the bloodstream that way you see. Then, as they get dopey, the rest is swallowed and absorbed and broken down slowly by the stomach acids. So they get an initial hit of painkiller and then a slow release that should sustain them until they get to a secondary care facility, to the hospital. When their arm flops down, then we know that they have taken it all. It can help take their mind off their injury, give them or a comrade something to do whilst we crack on treating their injuries. I just wish we'd had it in time for some of the casualties I'd treated.'

'So it must make your equipment lighter? No more of those auto-injections of morphine you once told me about. I never know how you manage to carry those big packs on your backs; you squaddies are like pack horses sometimes.'

'Sadly not, we still need them in case of facial injuries or if there is a risk that the casualty can choke,' replied Scott. 'So my job for the next few weeks is to go around the UK, training medics, all soldiers and officers, on how to use their oral transmucosal fentanyl citrate packs. That's the proper name for the lollipops. By next year all military personnel will be proficient in either self-administering it or applying them to wounded or injured troops. It's quite a responsibility. Every time someone is deployed they'll have at least two issued. Our wars and peace-keeping duties are getting more brutal, our enemies are devils and we need to keep on top of the game to protect ourselves. Working on the Medical Emergency Response Team really opened my eyes and I want to get back to doing that. This is an ideal foot in the door for me.'

'Geez oh son and all I do is move buses around like a boring board game.'

'No, don't say that dad. People rely on you to get them to school, work, University or to see their pals. No job is unimportant, without you the local hospitals wouldn't have staff arriving on time. Our future nurses and doctors wouldn't get to class on time to learn their skills.'

Douglas puffed up his chest once more, 'You know I've never looked at it like that before, thanks son.' He reached across and patted Scott's arm paternally. 'You're a good boy, you ken?'

'Aye dad, but I'm just as lucky to have you in my corner. And don't forget you've promised me a tour of your workplace someday soon.'

'Ha. Ha. I ken you only want to look around the building because it used to be an old barracks for the Gordons, but don't worry, I'd like to show you off tae ma work mates, there's some bonnie young quines there you know.'

'You can go off some people,' huffed Naomi under her breath, unheard by Scott.

'Does this lozenge thing work then, I'd hate to think of our brave boys and girls in pain after being shot at?'

'Really, really well dad, and ever so fast. It doesn't have too many side effects either, especially the sickness. With morphine we'd always have to give an extra injection of anti-nausea, but with the lollipop system it's not needed so much. It really is a clever bit of kit.'

'That's really good. You'll be good at teaching; you've a nice patient manner. I'm away to use the toilet, then we'll walk to the bus stop, aye?' He put down a couple of pound coins for Ronnie and Julie, more as a thank you for the free meals and drinks, though, as always, the service was great, even if she always made him blush.

'Here, let me leave a tip as well, I feel guilty taking free drinks and food,' said Scott as he reached into his pocket. As he put down a fiver, a piece of paper, caught up in the note, fell from his pocket. He quickly grabbed it from the table.

'What's that then?' asked Douglas, 'anything interesting?'

'No. Well not really,' replied Scott fiddling with the piece of paper, flipping it over and over, like turning a problem over in his mind.

'Sounds like you might want to tell me something?' enquired Douglas intuitively.

'Well, aye, but it's nae quite finished. I was going to make it neater and tidy it up for you first.'

'Oh,' encouraged Douglas to his son. 'Well, when you're ready.'

'If your bladder can hold on a minute longer, then I'll show you now,' said Scott as he unfolded the bit of paper. 'I've been trying my hand at poetry, you know, like mum used to do.'

'Fit rare! She wrote some beautiful poems. I'd often wondered over the years if you'd inherit her gift.'

'I'd have welcomed that gift,' said Scott cryptically to his unsuspecting father. 'My therapist thought that putting down on paper my thoughts and feelings might help. I know many soldiers have written their accounts of our wars, but I wanted to do something a bit different from an autobiography. So I thought I'd write poetry instead. It was more difficult than I thought it would be and I littered my flat floor with lots of scraps of torn paper. But I think this draft is okay.'

'Go on then, read it out, before we get kicked out for over-staying our welcome,' encouraged Douglas.

Scott cleared his throat and began reading tentatively, though he knew the words by heart:

'I have gently held the hand of a new born bairn as I helped breathe life into its delicate lungs,

But also grasped many hands of the dying as they took their last breath and thought of their mums,

As they hoped, prayed or screamed for loved ones they were about to leave,

Knowing that those left behind will mourn deeply and grieve,

For sons and daughters laid dying on a foreign floor,

Their duty done; pain borne no more.'

Douglas reached out for his son's hands, tears were forming in his eyes, and in a croaky voice he encouraged Scott, 'Go on son, read some more please.' As if to emphasise his words he let go of his son's hands and then patted the one holding the piece of paper. He sat back in his chair, ready to listen to his son.

Scott continued in a clearer and more confident voice:

'Stand easy soldier, your country is proud,

With honour your body will have a flag for a shroud,

Comrades will raise their rifles in the air,

And fire three volleys whilst saying a silent prayer,

For their brother or sister in arms,

Loved through the thickest of violent military storms.'

Scott lowered his piece of paper and carefully folded it. 'I'm not sure about the end sentence though,' he modestly said as he looked shocked to see his dad crying for the first time since his wife, Scott's beloved mother, had died. And that was the only time he'd seen his dad cry, until now.

'That's truly moving Scott,' he said reaching into his pocket for a tissue. He then wiped his eyes and blew his nose. 'Sorry loon must be auld age, I just think of all the Scott's who didn't come home and think myself so lucky to have you. I know we lost Naomi, and I think of all the other mums and dads who didn't get their children home. She, bless her, may have lost her family at such a young age, but we, her new family, grieved so much for her.'

'I know you miss her too dad,' said Scott who thought it bizarre that he could see Naomi right in front of him, resting her head on Douglas' shoulders, that orange glow now ablaze with brightness. 'She always thought of us and the Royal Army Medical Corps as her family. The RAMC Association gave her such a great send off and buried her, or what was left of her, with great honour and dignity. I just wish I'd been able to attend,' said Scott wistfully.

'You were still on the ventilator son; don't carry that guilt with you, she'd have wanted you to move on and be happy. Even though you fight our wars, you are all someone's child. And you are definitely your mother's child, you've her sensitive nature Scott, and she'd be affa proud of you ma laddie, very proud. Now excuse this sentimental auld fool afore he pees himself.'

Scott coughed in an effort to clear his own emotion. What a night this was turning out to be, he thought. 'No bother dad, take your time,' replied a happy Scott, relieved that his first poem went so well. Taking out his iPhone he continued as his father walked to the bathroom, 'There's someone I've been dying to talk with.'

Chapter 12

'It truly is you, isn't it?' asked a nervous Scott, still a little bit unsure at his good fortune, hoping beyond hope that he was correct. He was holding his mobile up to his ear as if deep in conversation. He hoped it didn't ring in the meantime and give away his deception. He did not want others in the restaurant or at the bar to think him crazy enough to be talking to himself. He knew that no-one but him could see his beloved Naomi.

'Yes Scott,' laughed Naomi joyfully with a small giggle, like a teenager on a first date, 'it really is me. I've been trying to tell you all along, it's really me.'

A solitary tear formed in the corner of Scott's right eye. It trickled slowly down his nose and onto his cheek, betraying his emotion, though no betrayal was needed. Naomi could see how overjoyed he was. Scott reached out with his free hand and cupped it around to where her face was. Though he knew he could not touch her he could somehow feel the heat of her iridescent glow, it was bright orange. 'But how, why, how is this possible, how and why are you here?' he spluttered out in an effort to make the most of their time alone before his father returned.

'I've come back to help you Scott, back from the spiritual world, from heaven if you like. The departure of the Grey Lady from this astral plain left a void that can only be filled by another spirit. Me. I was chosen, as you were gifted.'

'And you won't leave me will you, I couldn't bear to say goodbye to you again,' he begged.

'No Scott, you need me, remember what Jake said, and Jim. Their time with you was short, and only so much that needed to be said, that needed to be explained, could be said. Remember the Grey Lady's urgency, as she tried to quickly convey to you what your gift was...'

'What, wait,' interrupted a puzzled Scott. 'You'd left me by then, you'd gone off with the 453. You were one with them, one of them. I was alone with her; how could you possibly know that?'

'I've been with you always Scott, since then and before. I watched over you as Padre Caldwell and Major Dunn took you to the psychiatric ward to keep you safe. They didn't understand and luckily you did not share details of your gift with them or anyone. I have waited until you were strong once more and could accept my presence. Together we have much to do.'

Over in the bar Ronnie and Julie looked across to Scott talking on his mobile, his right arm raised. 'Looks like an affa heated conversation Scott's having. His arm is slowly moving around as if to emphasise his words. Hope everything is alright. He obviously didn't want his dad to hear this conversation,' noted Julie.

'Och, it's nice tae see faither an son sae close. An you ye cheeky imp should lay aff teasing Douglas. We didnae need a red traffic licht outside faun his face goes bright red fae your teasing.'

'Well, he is quite dishy for an auld man; I see where Scott gets his good looks from. I ken I cannae do it tae him, he's still grieving for his dead fiancée, a'body kens that, poor soul. But look at that smile on his face; I've never seen him so happy. Maybe he's had an update report on the mannie that fell aff the stage.'

'Much to do?' reflected Scott to Naomi.

'I'm afraid so haggis muncher, we've been teamed up; like in the best Hollywood films, me and you are going ghostie hunting!'

'What, like Ghostbusters? Do I get a special uniform and backpack with special gun?'

Naomi laughed her infectious giggle, 'No you stupid nursey, not quite like that, but we do need to work together, to bring the spiritual from the physical, that's why we need each other, and why we were chosen.'

'By God? You know I don't believe in a God, none of them, not anymore,' replied Scott, now looking downcast.

'But you must for this to work, for us to stay together. He has pre-ordained this, our being together. It was all part of his plan for us, me dying and then being permitted to return to you. I know what happened to your mother was awful. So was what happened to my parents on the autobahn, but it all happened for a reason, trust me, and trust in God,' pleaded Naomi.

'Have you seen her, is my mother in heaven?' questioned Scott urgently. He looked up to see his father returning from the bathroom. He looked at Naomi, who was silent again. Scott reluctantly withdrew his hand, sadly, like an illicit lover having to leave a brief tryst. He took his phone from his ear and pretended to touch the screen, as if to end a call.

'I hope that actor fellow was alright, Scott doesn't look so happy now, he looks deeply worried,' remarked Julie to Ronnie.

'Och, yer an affa gossip quine, I'm awa tae check the cellar,' said an exasperated Ronnie.

Julie looked around the bar and restaurant, it was empty, save for Douglas and Scott, the Aberdeen dreich and windy weather always made folks go home early, there was no need to chuck out reluctant drinkers and diners tonight. There was equally no need to dim the lights or turn off the music. 'I'll chase those twa oot then, and for once we can close in good time.' She looked back to see that she had been talking to herself, Ronnie had long gone. She walked around the bar, making her way to father and son, just as Douglas got back to the table, but before he could sit down and get comfortable.

'Who was that on the phone son, anyone interesting?' enquired Douglas.

Just as Scott was about to make up an excuse he was thankfully saved the trouble by Julie who interrupted with, 'Is that you twa loons aff then?' Before they could answer she continued with, 'I'll go and get your coat handsome, you'll need to wrap your body around something warm tonight, it's affa cauld oot there,' she said suggestively.

Douglas warmed from the heat radiating from his face. He went even brighter as Julie held out his coat in such a way that made it clear that she was to help him on with it. As he reluctantly put his arms back and slid into his coat, Julie pulled it over his shoulders and smoothed down the fabric, slowly and delectably, 'there lover boy, that'll keep you snug as a rug!'

'Aye, well, er, thanks lass,' faltered Douglas as he fumbled with his buttons, much to Scott's mirth. He looked across to Naomi who had her hand on her forehead as if to say 'Enough! Get a room you two.' Scott wondered if he should ask about his mum again, once he got Naomi alone. It wouldn't be sensible to be seen by Aberdeen's finest, patrolling the streets weary of drunken revellers, to be seen talking to himself. He'd soon be helped into another type of jacket. He'd have to wait until they got home and dad had gone to bed. He hoped Naomi would stay with him and would follow him home.

Chapter 13

Douglas picked up his empty mug, 'I'm awa tae ma bed son, have a good night's sleep,' he said, hoping, for his son's sake, that Scott would not suffer any nightmares tonight. He was pleased to have such understanding neighbours.

'Aye dad thanks for a nice night out, well, except for what happened to Calum.'

'Aye,' replied Douglas, 'I ken fit ye meant,' he patted his stomach, 'two lovely meals, night son, dinnae bide up too late watching telly.'

'Ah'm nae 12 years' auld dad!' joked Scott, 'Night dad.' He moved across the room and embraced his father, holding him tighter than normal. 'I love you dad.'

Douglas moved back from the embrace and looked into his son's eyes and with a heartfelt voice said 'I love you too son, take care driving won't you? It's been great seeing you again, I hope you get leave again soon, perhaps we can go on holiday somewhere together?'

'Aye, I'd like that dad.'

'Well, I'll be off to bed, I've an early start in the morning, you enjoy a lie in before your long drive.' Douglas left their lounge and closed the door behind him. Scott listened out for the chink of the mug on the kitchen draining board and the light step of his dad's feet on the staircase. Satisfied, he switched off the television and turned to Naomi, who had been watching them silently from the sofa, like an invigilator at a school exam.

'Is this how it is to be, me waiting to be alone before I can speak to you Naomi?' asked Scott, moving across to the sofa.

'Only if you don't want to be carted off to the funny farm again!' she replied sarcastically, playfully trying to thump his arm.

'Talking of which, I've hundreds of questions, but most of all I think I'd like to know if I imagined you at my flat in Aldershot. You know, when the Grey Lady was taking me to places like France, showing me what she lived through during World War One. Were you there and in the clock tower? And in my flat, looking after me when I took ill?' garbled Scott, getting the questions out just in time as his mind raced with all the questions he wanted to ask her, tumbling out of him like a sprung coil slinky toy.

'Whoa cowboy! Take a breath, steady on. Okay, yes, I've been with you since I was killed. I've watched over you when you were injured and then through the induced coma. I was with you every step of the way at the hospital in Birmingham. For every tentative step you took on the road to recovery, I was there too, walking by your side, but hidden. I knew you would not be able to cope with seeing me, your body and mind was so fragile. Even at Headley Court you looked so vulnerable.'

'So none of this has been my imagination, I've not been going crazy,' sighed Scott with relief.

'No darling, no, you have not. You have been chosen because of your strength, not because of your physical strength, but for your inner strength. Few would have coped with all you have seen and done, tonight is testimony to that. You've probably wondered why you've seen so many ghosts.'

'Just a bit! Blimey, could I have seen any more! Interesting all the same, though Jake's head coming off was a bit grisly.'

'Yes,' continued Naomi, 'it was all a demonstration, to you, that you could cope, that you are better. That you have this wonderful gift.'

'So why did you leave me when the Grey Lady left with Hugh?' questioned Scott. 'I needed you, more than ever.'

'Your mind was not ready Scott. It was not open to possibilities. You thought you had created the Grey Lady and I as a defensive illusion, as part of your Post Traumatic Stress Disorder, when in fact it was me being laid to rest that was the delusion.'

'So the Grey Lady was real?' asked Scott.

'Yes she was, she did need to tell you her story. That is your gift, you have the power to find military ghosts and hear their stories. Then we lay them to rest.'

'We?' questioned Scott.

'Yes, my love, we, us together. Some are not going to go easily, you need my spiritual help, think of me as your guiding angel…'

'Like a guardian angel,' interrupted Scott.

'Not quite Scott, those keep you safe, my job is to help you understand and to take you to where you need to be, like a spirit guide.'

'So there are angels in the world?' asked an incredulous Scott. 'I can't believe that, with what I've seen, all the pain and suffering.'

'You have to believe Scott, you need your faith, we have much horror in front of us, Jake and Jim were lovely men in life, but there are monsters and demons ahead of us. The evillest of men and women when they were alive do not change in the after-life, nor are they accepted into heaven,' replied Naomi. 'Many evil spirits still torment the living.'

'But mum's suffering was so needless, she was in such pain. She tried not to show it, but I knew she was. So did dad, we looked on helplessly. That's when I lost my faith. How could a caring God do this to the loveliest person I knew? That's why I later became a nurse; I wanted to help ease people's suffering. If only I could have got off that helicopter, I could have saved you.'

'No Scott, no. We've been through this at your flat, move on from your survivor's guilt; listen to your therapist.

'Were you there too; at each session?' said Scott mildly irritated at what should have been private.

'Yes darling, I walked with you; each step of the way remember.' replied Naomi placing her hand above Scott's, the orange glow calming him.

Scott looked confused, 'but there were two of you.'

Now it was Naomi's turn to look puzzled, 'two of me?'

'No,' said Scott, 'sorry, this is all a bit strange, it's so much to take in and I have so many things I want to say to you, to ask you.'

'I mean there were two ghosts, you and the Grey Lady, at the same time. Only you weren't at the same time. You both kept missing each other, then you had that confusing fight, then you made up, then you both left. It was all a bit Twilight Zoney. It was so much to take in. Losing you again wrenched my heart in two. I love you Naomi.'

She placed her hands over Scott's cheeks, 'And I love you too, so very much. Let me try to explain things Scott. The Grey Lady, Morag, needed you to see what she had been through in life, as did I. She could not move on until you'd understood and we'd both borne witness to her life and dramatic death. Only then could she be reunited with Hugh and find peace. It was difficult for her to relinquish her caring role after the Cambridge Military Hospital was closed. She had no patients to look after, no souls to help to the after-life. It confused her and unbalanced her spiritual mind. That is why she manifested to you so horribly at first.'

'And you,' asked Scott, still desperately trying to understand, 'why were you there, why did you keep coming and going?'

'Think of it as a type of handover, like when you nurses take over a shift. Though all the patient notes, scan results and blood test results are there, it would take you hours to read through. Instead, you report to each other the necessary information to enable you to take over their treatments and get the jobs done, to care.'

Scott gave a protracted 'Okay' as he tried to assimilate this information. 'I think I'm beginning to understand. In her own way, she was training you.'

'If you like, yes,' confirmed Naomi.

'So how does this work? Do we go out in the middle of the night looking for ghosts?' tentatively asked Scott, who loved his sleep.

'Ha, no you lummox head. You've been watching too many James Wan films. Well, not always in the middle of the night and most of them will come to you. He has been trying to reach out to you, but you must go to him,' said Naomi cryptically.

'You mean Jake?' asked Scott.

'No, he's happy where he is in his treasured Theatre. That's his peace made, I mean the loud noises.'

'You mean you hear them too, it's not me going crazy again?' Scott latched onto this idea hopefully; they were getting noisier and more intrusive. He was finally glad to share them.

'Not as loud as you, but yes, it's a spirit trying to reach out to you. But your faith is stopping you from seeing him. Or rather it's your lack of faith. You need to believe, Scott.'

'I'll try, but how do I know this is not just in my imagination again?'

'Trust me Scott, I'm really here and won't be going anywhere without you.

We need each other, more than ever,' warned Naomi in a whisper.

Chapter 14

'What was that you said Naomi? I'm afraid I've heard too many rounds go off in the heat of battle without having time to be able to put in earplugs. The same with roaring Chinook engines; it's made me a bit deaf at times,' said Scott absently poking his finger into his ear, his mind whizzing and whirring with so many thoughts and questions like a demented and out of control electronic toy racing car running around a room, going around in circles and bumping off skirting boards to be left spinning and cavorting in the middle of the floor.

'Nothing sweetie, I just said that it's time you went to bed, like your dad said, you have a long drive ahead of you,' replied Naomi gently, hoping to calm his thoughts down.

Scott looked puzzled, 'how do you know it's a long drive, do you know where I'm planning on going?'

Naomi laughed, 'No need to be so paranoid, I really have been with you at all times. I know everything. And it is about time that you visited him,' she gently chided. 'It's long overdue.'

Scott ignored the rebuke, he'd only just thought of visiting him this evening, during the resuscitation. He'd made up his mind to visit an old, neglected friend. 'Then it's just as well I don't have any embarrassing secrets then, isn't it!' joked Scott in an attempt to take her mind off a painful subject, he felt ever so guilty at not being able to bring himself to see someone who well deserved a visit and his friendship.

'Well, other than your military nursing collection, have you been out and about, scouring junk shops for smelly old bedpans lately?' laughed Naomi, going along with the diversion. She knew Scott was already kicking himself and punishing himself for far too long neglecting to rekindle an old friendship.

'If you are all seeing then why don't you know?' quizzed Scott.

'I know you haven't Scott, that's why I know how upset you've been, how worried about your mental health you have become. Don't feel guilty about enjoying life. You need to be like Julie, start to laugh again, do the things you enjoy, like your obsession with all things about military history, read books, watch films, spend time with other people, make new friends.' Naomi hesitated briefly knowing that one day she would have to painfully let him go physically, 'learn to love again Scott.'

'Up until now it has all seemed so pointless, so futile, without you, my love.'

'I know darling, but I'm not going anywhere, not without you, not until…'

'I die?' replied Scott, 'or join you in heaven, if there really is such a place, like what happened to Hugh and Morag.

'There really is such a place Scott, it may not be all harps and clouds like some people believe, but those who love each other are reunited in places where they want to be, and with whom, places of fondness, places that matter.'

'Mmm,' replied a sceptical Scott, 'I wish I could truly believe that. I mean I saw the light that guided Morag, The Grey Lady, to her beloved Hugh, the Gordon Highlander soldier from World War One, but they simply vanished before my very eyes. I didn't see a bright light or pearly gates, or angels on clouds. So where have they gone?'

Naomi smiled, 'if only you knew Scott,' she thought! 'They are together Scott, where they need to be, in their idea of heaven. You really need to believe Scott, just like Mulder and Scully in the X-Files TV series. And now you really need to get to bed, you need your sleep.'

'But I have so many questions I need to ask you Naomi,' replied Scott hurriedly. He started to ramble, his words almost not getting out of his mouth quick enough. 'Do you even need sleep? What do you do when I sleep? Will you still be here when I wake up? I can't bear to lose you again, please tell me I'm not imagining you being here, making up this conversation in my head…'

Naomi interrupted Scott's negative thoughts by placing her outstretched fingers of her right hand to Scott's lips. He felt that warm fuzzy calming sensation again that interrupted his flow of questions and slowed his thoughts and left him mindfully at peace. She moved her left hand up and formed her index finger to her lips as she said 'Shhhh. There will be plenty of time to learn more about this wonderful experience we are to share for the rest of your life. I promise you I am not going anywhere,' she said in earnest, hoping Scott would relax and trust her. 'I don't want to be anywhere else, but by your side. But for now I think you need to get some sleep. I bet your body is crying out for rest after the adrenaline slump from tonight's activities?' She nodded her head knowingly, having experienced the fatigue that hits you like a hammer's head to the face, straight after emergency care, soon after the casualty is removed safely from your responsibility and onto another's shoulders.

'Aye, too right. Okay I'll go along with this, but just one more question?' requested a playful Scott, his broad infectious grin back on his face.

'Alright, as long as you then climb the wooden stairs to Bedfordshire sleepy nursey,' said Naomi, teasingly.

'I'm bursting for the toilet, could we please have a no bathroom manifesting rule!' pleaded a rather shy Scott with a red face, a trait he'd inherited from his father.

Chapter 15

Scott climbed the stairs as quietly as he could. He felt it was like being on night manoeuvres in basic training, learning not to make a sound, least the enemy should hear it and start firing. Only on this occasion he was hoping not to awaken his dad, who needed his sleep before his early shift in the morning. As he crept past his dad's room he couldn't help feeling like a lover on a sleepover at the parent's house, moving furtively across the landing for some illicit fun and naughtiness. He just hoped that Naomi would be there, that he had not imagined her reappearance back into his life. He elongated his stride, knowing that that particular part of the carpet gave way to a creaking floorboard underneath. He opened his bedroom door and was met with the reassuring orange light that he had come to learn meant that Naomi was happy, that meant that he was loved by her. He now put aside all doubts and shed them as he walked into his bedroom, prepared for this new exciting chapter of his life. Thank you Jake, he thought, you wonderful man, you have your beloved theatre, and now I have my beloved Naomi, my Hugh to Morag; all is well in the world thought Scott, and long may it last.

He silently closed the door so as not to awaken his sleeping father, feeling the bite of the snub make contact with the doorframe. He wanted it shut properly so that if dad got up through the night to relieve his aching bladder of more of the two pints he drank, he would not hear him talking to Naomi. He had so many questions to ask of her.

He turned around; no need for lights with the amber glow that lit up his airfix models that surrounded his childhood bedroom. Planes and helicopters hung down from the ceiling as if in flight across a cloudless white sky whilst display cabinets were full of tanks, jeeps, army trucks and small delicately painted soldiers. As a child building and painting these helped to take his mind off his lonely grieve for his mother whilst forging a lifetime love for the military. He was always destined to be in the army, but little did his younger self know just how deep that love would go, what sacrifices would be made and what a special gift he would receive from such gut wrenching and utter heartbreak.

Scott smiled at his beloved Naomi, years of emotional pain forgotten in a heartbeat. He was back in the house where he felt safest; with the two people he loved the most.

'See, nursey, you should have a little faith. I'm still here. I hope you washed your hands and brushed your teeth,' she teased.

'Aye, lass, but I'm not ready for sleeping just yet. I've lots of questions,' replied Scott as he took off his shirt and laid it over the back of a chair. He started unzipping his jeans, feeling an odd sort of loss that the belt, now covered in blood and most probably lying in a yellow bagged bin in casualty, was gone from his life. He smiled. He now had the most wonderful present in the world back in his life.

As if knowing what he was thinking Naomi said, 'I paid a fortune for that belt!'

'Ha ha, you really do know what I'm thinking,' retorted Scott as he slipped off his jeans and threw them over his shirt. He made a mental note to put them into the washing machine in the morning. Dad wouldn't mind washing them for him and he'd collect them the next time he came back on leave. Going on holiday with him seemed a great idea. Perhaps somewhere abroad? He looked at Naomi who was laid on his bed, trying to pat it and inviting him to join her. He wondered if she would join them on a plane if they went overseas, or fly her own way there like the spirits in the air in his favourite film Scrooge with Albert Finney.

'I'll go first class and leave you boys cramped up in economy seats,' she joked, still trying to pat the duvet. 'Mmm, I've missed that figure; you've been working out more.'

Scott felt unabashed at his dead fiancée seeing his body and he was quickly getting used to her mindreading abilities. With a swift movement he removed his boxer shorts and jumped across to the bed to join her.

Naomi felt like a worried teenager hoping not to be interrupted by her parents during the amorous advances of her boyfriend and shushed him for the second time that night. 'Do you want to wake your dad up you daftie. Now lie still and keep your voice down.'

'Sorry, got a bit over-excited there. It's just wonderful having you back in my life again. I feel like I'm 18 years old and on top of the world. Who knew that I'd have you in my bed again? It's just fantastic. I thought I'd lost you forever and yet here you are. Maybe there is a heaven after all.' Scott interrupted his own chain of thought and looking fretful, 'I haven't died have I? Is this my idea of heaven being in bed with you again?'

Naomi laughed, 'well we were rather good together weren't we lover boy? But in all seriousness, no, you haven't died. I really am back.' Sounding more serious now, she continued with, 'I'm your spirit guide. My role is to bridge the gap in your understanding between the dead and the living. I interact with the spirits who aren't quite ready to show themselves to you until such times as you understand how to communicate with them, understand and then lay them to rest.'

'Sounds easy partner,' drawled Scott, failing at a cowboy impression.

Naomi groaned, 'I'd forgotten how terrible you were at impressions. But seriously, you need to listen, because you still haven't worked out the noises yet, have you. He's trying to communicate with you.'

Scott's face fell, 'you mean the sudden violent drumming beats I can hear, repetitively reverberating around my head?'

'Yes. Only they are not in your head Scott. They are real. He is trying to communicate with you.'

'Who?' Scott asked eagerly, relieved again to learn he hadn't been going mad, hearing noises in his head.

'I think it better that you learn your new skills for yourself Scott, you are going to have to learn quickly because something truly evil is growing stronger.'

'Okay Obi-Wan Kenobi!'

Naomi groaned again and tried to hit Scott, forgetting that sadly she could not make contact. 'Enough with the Star Wars jokes, and don't you dare say anything about using the force, or may the force be with you. This is serious because not all ghosts are going to be as sweet as he is, or fun like Jake, or looking for peace like Jim.' Seeing the shock appear on his face she quickly continued, 'Yes, I was with you at Erskine, watching with pride. You did well picking up so quickly what Jim's needs were. But he was a sweet old man, others won't be. The Grey Lady didn't have time to explain, nor could Jim, and I don't think you are quite ready to face him yet, and fortunately we do have some months before he manifests himself. So let's just concentrate on one ghost at a time. There shouldn't be any more multiple manifestations, that was just me preparing you for seeing me again. Sorry about that. I just needed to know that you had the mental strength to accept me.'

'I do,' replied an elated Scott. He reached out to try and stroke Naomi's face. I just wish that I could touch and feel you, to kiss and cuddle you, to make love to you.'

'As do I Scott, as do I,' she sighed. 'We'll talk about this another day, when you are ready to listen. It's been quite a day for you and you really need to sleep.'

'I ken quine, but I'm too over-excited to sleep. I feel like a young laddie again on Christmas Eve, eagerly awaiting Santa to deliver my presents for being good.'

Naomi looked around her and laughed. 'Aye, though I think you've enough toys already. 'You've accepted that I truly am here?'

'Aye, lass, I have,' replied Scott in earnest.

'And that we'll always be together, no matter what and that I'm not going anywhere?'

'Aye!'

'Then trust me, I'll help you sleep, and when you wake up I'll still be here.'

'Okay,' replied Scott, eagerly wondering what she had in mind.

'Then get under the duvet properly, lie back and settle down as if to sleep with me by your side.'

Scott obeyed and laid himself out down the length of the bed, his head gently bounced onto his pillows as he drew his winter warming duvet around him. He smiled peacefully as he remembered that he always used to lie on his back whilst in bed with Naomi, so that she could snuggle up to him. He used to enjoy wrapping his arms around her, making her feel protected and safe. How he missed that he thought.

'Close your eyes Scott,' whispered Naomi, who sounded just near to his left ear. 'Feel yourself relax. Breath in and out and concentrate on your breathing. Take a few long slow breaths in and out.'

As Scott complied he was unaware that Naomi was stood over him, rubbing her hands into an orangey ember fury that then leapt from her body and into his, like a spark from a coal fire suddenly spitting out onto a hearth rug. He could feel intense warmth along his naked body as Naomi, now ablaze with a fierce glow settled down along the length of him, trying to engulf him with her glowing body.

Scott sighed long and slowly, feeling all his muscle tension relax into the mattress as the last of his long slow breaths escaped his lungs. He could almost smell her, run his fingers through her soft black hair and stroke her fringe aside as he ran his fingers slowly and softly down to her cheek. He inhaled and drawing far into the inner depths of his memory he could smell her aromas of perfume and femininity. Their bodies finally touched and Scott mentally clenched his eyes tighter least the spell become broken. He so wanted her and could finally feel their bodies become one as they gently rocked together and sang the music of love as they reached a sole-sharing climax unlike any physical one he'd ever had before. He wanted to shout out her name, as a mantra of his love, but an incredible peace shone throughout his body as Naomi shared and bared her very essence with him and with a final shudder and sigh Scott fell asleep to the sound of a whispered 'I love you' that repeated itself like the gentle ebb and flow of a tide at sunset. The orange glow faded away to blackness like the dying ember of an untended fire.

Chapter 16

The teasing winter sun shone through the curtains enticing Scott to stir. He stretched out luxuriously, like a cat lying on its favourite armchair, showing its owner all four extended paws. He gave a loud prolonged yawn. 'That was incredible Naomi, I've had such a great sleep, I can't remember the last time I slept the night through. I don't know what you did to me, but it was just wonderful.'

Scott waited a few moments, but received no reply, just the gentle far off cawing of seagulls in the air, flying around, eagle-eyed, seeking their next opportune meal. He felt afraid to open his eyes; he'd fooled himself again, hadn't he? It was another living fantasy, one more ridiculous waking illusion. Och well, he thought whilst keeping his eyes shut. He tentatively whispered, 'Naomi?'

He still received no reply. As his full senses returned, he remembered that his father would now be at work. He reluctantly opened his eyes, for now he would have to face up to the stark reality; he was mad and he could tell no-one about his flights of fantasy for fear of returning into psychiatric care. He'd only just been able to hang onto his career in the army and doubted his Matron and Commanding Officer would be so understanding a second time. How could he convince them that he was taking his medicines and complying with psychotherapy and group support meetings whilst seeing and interacting with dead people? 'Naomi, are you there,' said Scott, a little louder and in a plaintive voice.

He listened out to the silence which even the seagulls could not penetrate. It pierced through his ears and stabbed into his heart engulfing him; he was alone, metaphorically and figuratively. He pulled his duvet closer to him, wrapped it around his shoulders, not for warmth, but for comfort, as if he could cocoon himself away from reality. He shut his eyes tight this time and drew his knees up to his chest. Tears pricked his eyes and slowly rolled down the sides of his nose like drops from an icicle. He felt cold to the core; and so, so alone. He inhaled deeply and felt himself shudder as a heartfelt sigh escaped from his nose whilst forcing his shoulders to relax. I'm not going mad again, he thought, I'm sane, I know I am. But yet I probably look like the stereotypical mad man lying in bed, cradling himself away from the world: and talking to himself. He pulled the duvet off, as if shedding the image whilst pulling himself together. "Okay soldier boy, up and at 'em," as one of his sergeants used to enjoy saying to his charges. Using his index fingers, he dried his tears and remembered that he had someone special to visit today, and a long drive ahead of him.

Scott reached into his chest of drawers and pulled out a fresh t-shirt, sweater and underwear and stepped across to the wardrobe for a pair of jeans. As he dressed he continued to glance around, hoping she would manifest. She didn't. He sighed again as he bundled up his blood stained clothes from last night and sighed further when he opened the curtains and could see in daylight just how blood splattered and soiled his trainers were. He reached into his opened suitcase and took out his shoes and slipped them on. The trainers would have to go in the wash too, but back at his own flat: along with the stained clothing; he really couldn't expect his dad to wash these, not now that he'd seen just how soiled they were. He popped them in an empty carrier bag, 5p from the local shop and his contribution to charity, threw it into the suitcase, zipped it up and wheeled it to the door. As he made the bed he couldn't resist bending over to smell the duvet and pillow. There was nothing, no scent. She had not been there. Another sigh escaped his nostrils as he looked around his childhood bedroom once more; his shoulders drooped further with the inevitability of it all and he left without turning back.

"There are fresh tattie scones in the breadbin Scott, take care, Dad xx.' Scott carefully folded the note and popped it into his jeans back pocket whilst helping himself to the flat morning treat that looked like slightly thick white and black triangular pancakes. He loved these, especially with beans and black pudding, but he couldn't face all that this morning, not with his heavy heart. Instead he popped them in the toaster so that they turned ochre coloured, removed them and spread them with butter. As he chewed he pondered the wonder of someone inventing these tasty breakfast treats that were made from mashed potatoes, plain flour, butter and salt. They certainly made for a filling start to the day.

He moved over to the kitchen window to better hear the gentle cooing of dad's pigeons. He'd always loved the soothing sound of their fluttering wings as they moved from the shed through to their perches in the aviary section of the pigeon loft. He could just picture her there, inside, cradling dad's prized pigeons, whispering to them, telling them how beautiful they were. A brief smile spread across his face as he remembered the first time she had seen the one-way system of the sputnik trap which allowed the pigeons to fly back into the loft, without being able to get back out. She had laughed as each popped a head through the wooden bars, as if to test for safety and looked around for predators, and then plopped down, gave a funny bum shake of the feathers, before flying elegantly through to the safety of the shed. Naomi couldn't get enough of letting them out of the trap door each morning, seeing them fly around the neighbourhood in close circular pack formation, like a tight configuration of an aeronautical display by the Red Arrows, before gracefully landing on the ledge of the wooden sputnik trap. His smile vanished along with the fading memory. He turned back, resolved to attempt to move on, to struggle and put this experience behind him, to try and live his life the best way he could; without her.

Chapter 17

The gears crunched in protest like a roaring rhinoceros as Scott, angry now at his foolishness of last night, slammed them into second as he slowed down for yet another set of traffic lights on the A90. This Dundee bypass was always a pain to get around. He missed the long stretch between Aberdeen and past Stonehaven where he could just put his foot down and take his rage out by speeding through the Scottish countryside.

RUBIDUB DUM, RUBIDUB DUM, blasted around the car. 'NOT NOW!' yelled Scott. 'I DON'T KNOW WHAT YOU WANT FROM ME! LEAVE ME ALONE!' He turned on his CD player and cranked up the volume to drown out the intrusive drumming noise. The sounds of local Doric country style singer Colin Clyne belted out his hit Doin' Fine, from his album, The Never Ending Pageant. It instantly soothed his irritability at his own stupidity as he passed the final roundabout and sped beyond the Shell station, finally out of Dundee and onwards to Perth and further south. He grimaced wryly at the lyrics which cut straight to his heart, as if the singer had written the song just for him:

Take that bullet from out of my stomach

Put it right back into your gun, I no longer want it

Cause I'm over you, I'm over you

And I'm doin' fine.

Only he wasn't. His gear shifts became much smoother as he tried to relax back into his seat and pressed his foot onto the accelerator until he reached 70 miles per hour. Even in his rage he didn't want to speed above the limit. Instead he banged his fist against the steering wheel.

'Alright there haggis muncher? What's put you in such a bad mood? Hope you're stopping for a bacon buttie and coffee at The Horn?' asked Naomi, who had suddenly appeared from nowhere onto the seat beside him, as if teleported down from space in an episode of Blake's 7.

'What the f…' screeched out Scott in his shock at her sudden manifestation which caused him to swerve his car towards the outside lane. He was grateful that it was fortuitously empty; he valued his clean licence and narrowly escaped having it taken from him after his head injury and rehabilitation.

'Naughty, naughty nursey, remember your no swearing rule!'

Scott pulled the car back to his lane, quickly checking that there were no cameras capturing his driving error. He turned down the music and while trying to keep one eye on the road, he turned to Naomi quickly and said in a controlled voice, 'you are in my imagination, and I'm going to ignore you until you go away.' He then turned the music back up, just as Colin was singing the chorus from his next song, My Bonny Broken Valentine. Scott gave a sardonic smile as he heard *"Oh I love you even though it don't look like I care."*

'Don't be such a sulk, and keep your eyes on the road. Are you cross because I left you?' probed Naomi.

Scott hesitated, should he have a conversation with the imaginary Naomi and get dragged further into a fantasy world? He relented, only because he knew people seeing him as they passed in their cars would think he was singing along to his music, rather than talking to a dead lassie. He turned Colin's singing down again. 'You lied,' he said crossly, almost like a child. 'You said you'd always be by my side, that you'd never leave me. But you weren't there when I woke up.'

'Ha, ha, are you feeling all used after a one-night stand?'

'No. It was lovely what you did to me, I slept so well, but I woke up all lonely, where were you?'

'Look Scott, well maybe not look too long, I don't want you to crash the car. I really am here; we will be together always…'

'So where were you this morning?' interrupted Scott.

'You've a lot to learn Scott, but last night you needed a good night's sleep, especially since you've a long drive. So I transferred my energy force through to you, to help you achieve a heightened state of relaxation. I've never done it before and it drained me. I'm still learning about this gig, the Grey Lady taught me well, but I didn't learn everything I need to know. You need to have faith Scott, in me and in God.'

Scott harrumphed, 'aye, well, I'll have faith in you, but you ken I dinnae believe in God anymore.'

'I know Scott, but one day you will, you must, in your own time. Now stop sulking, it doesn't suit you.'

Scott was still looking ahead and had started to slow down. He pushed down his indicator and heard the tick tick noise as it filled the silence between them. He finally broke it and said, 'I thought I'd gone mad again, but you're really here, aren't you,' he asked hopefully.

'Yes Scott, I am, so stop sulking and treat yourself to the best bacon buttie in Scotland.'

Scott's grin returned as he pulled into the Horn roadside restaurant and parked near to the sign with the loudhailer. He hoped that when they moved down the road to the new £1 million development they'd take that and the cow statue from the roof. He rather liked the 1960s motorway café building as it was; there was something comforting about the old tables and chairs and linoleum floor. Going around the servery reminded him of being in old army canteens. He turned off the ignition and turned to her, 'What would I do without my scarlet woman, Naomi Scarlet.'

'Probably be carted off to the loonie farm Scott Grey,' she replied whilst returning the grin. 'We are going to have some great times together haggis muncher, but you know what I'm going to regret just now?'

'I dinnae ken lass, fit?' questioned Scott, looking a bit worried again.

'Not being able to eat those bacon butties, do they really deep fry the streaky bacon to give them that irresistible crunchy, salty taste in those soft Scottish morning rolls!'

'Nae telling, it's a Scot's secret, like Nessie! It's not nicknamed the A90 Behemoth for nothing!' teased Scott.

Ha, if you only knew about her too Scott, thought Naomi with a twinkle in her eyes.

Chapter 18

Later that evening Scott, with Naomi by his side, drove along the lime tree avenue towards Tedworth House, near the Hampshire and Wiltshire border. Though many of the trees had been pulled violently from their roots and destroyed in the great storms of October 1987 and January 1990, they still acted as tall guiding beacons, encouraging them on for this final part of their journey. They soon drew up to the magnificent white stoned mansion house that had been converted into a Help for Heroes recovery centre. The area would have been familiar to many soldiers who trained in the edges of Salisbury Plain. It was here that Scott had come to see a friend.

'Wow!' he exclaimed as he drove slowly past the bronze statue of two helmeted soldiers in full combat gear carrying a wounded comrade on a stretcher. 'That's an impressive bit of art; it really does capture what the RAMC and other Corps and Regiments did during Afghanistan.

Naomi looked proudly on, lost for words, as Scott parked his car in what would have been the courtyard and carriage porch which still had evident archways of this building that dated back to 1828, though the original building dated back even further.

Scott looked out of his windscreen, above the two storied building to its centre piece, a small clock tower with a weathervane above it. He couldn't help comparing it to the one near his flat, back in Aldershot. This one was not as grand, and had an open structure beneath the clock, certainly no room for captured Russian bells. Nor room to move around the clock tower either, he thought, thinking back to the sad final moments of Morag's life. He wondered why magnificent buildings like these always had such clocks, but then answered his own question by knowing that pocket watches in those days were just for the landed gentry and these clocks enabled their workers and servants to be on time. Bonnie all the same he thought.

'You don't know, do you?' asked Naomi, interrupting his thoughts.

'Eh,' replied Scott vaguely.

'No, you really don't, otherwise you'd have told me by now.'

'Eh,' repeated a confused Scott.

'This used to be the mess for the QA nursing sisters.'

'No way! Really, so where was Tidworth Military Hospital?'

'Just down the road,' she replied, surprised that Scott hadn't researched this old and important hospital, given its close proximity to one of the largest training grounds for British soldiers.

'But that's the barracks I'm due to stay at for the next few days whilst I teach them about...'

'Lollipops, I ask you, what's wrong with good old fashioned injections. In my day...'

Scott interrupted Naomi, 'so when was this used as a mess then?' He was eager to fill in his knowledge gap.

'Oh, when the hospital was opened in 1907, the Queen Alexandra's Imperial Military Nursing Service sisters moved in a few years later though. There were loads of barracks around here and they needed better nursing care. They were named after battles in India, you know the old Raj and British Empire, don't you know, what, what,' said Naomi in her best upper class posh voice.

'Your impressions are worse than mine, so what were they called then, Miss know it all?'

'Aliwal, Assaye, Bhurtpore, Candahar, Delhi, Jellalabad, Lucknow and Mooltan, or at least I think that's how they are pronounced.'

Scott looked impressed, she had never shown this much interest or knowledge of military history when she was alive. He only recognised Lucknow and Delhi barracks.

As if reading his thoughts, she continued, 'the first barracks opened in 1904, just a few years after the Secretary of War gained new powers to purchase or lease land due to the passing of the Military Lands Act. That's why the army now own so much of the area, it was considered handy for nearby Southampton, London and Aldershot. Hutted camps were soon built in nearby Bulford and then Larkhill, as the training needs increased. It became known as the second home of the British Army.'

Scott looked at her open mouthed.

'I know quite a lot now; I can even take you back in time, like the Grey Lady did. Only it zaps my energy too, like what I did last night, so I may disappear again.'

'Cool,' said Scott, 'I mean the back in time bit, not the disappearing bit. So when did Tidworth Military Hospital close?'

'1977, though the QAs didn't always live here in Tedworth House. They were deployed during the Second World War and the American's moved in, until they left for the D-Day landings. Though many came back for their wives, they married local women. The Commander of the British Troops in this area offered it to the wife of President Franklin D. Roosevelt. She started a Red Cross club for the American soldiers and soon Eleanor was supervising the cooking of hamburgers and the pouring of coffee. There were some RAMC medics using parts of the building at the time and they weren't too pleased to be sharing their accommodation with the Americans; especially when they started dating the Voluntary Aid Detachment ladies who were working in the hospital. Even that got took over by the Americans. Eleanor Roosevelt even employed some of them to run her Red Cross club. Apparently the Hokey-Cokey was invented here.'

'You made that last bit up,' laughed Scott.

'No, honest, all seeing and knowing, remember?'

Scott looked sceptical. 'So when did the QAs return to Tedworth House, and why's it not called Tidworth House?'

'You need to study English history a bit more Scott, many English villages had their names corrupted, misspelt and changed over the years. The area was really tiny centuries ago, and even in 1897 when buildings like this were sold to the War Office by owners like Sir John William Kelk, the population was only in the hundreds. Its original name was Tudanwyrth, then about a hundred years later it was recorded in the Domesday Book as Todeorde and then centuries later it was known as Tudewrth or Tuddeworth then eventually Tedeworth became Tedworth or Tidworth, both pronunciations were used.'

'I do know a bit about that, it's because most folk didn't read or write, many only learned to do so about the time of the Napoleonic War. So they learned how to say things from their families, hence the corruptions,' added Scott smugly.

Naomi felt mischievous, no less because she had been wanting to demonstrate her knowledge and now he was interrupting her again. 'Look into your rear view mirror,' she requested as her body began to glow orange.

Scott obeyed and was treated to the sight of a 1960s QA, now a member of the Queen Alexandra's Royal Army Nursing Corps, struggling in the wind to walk across the courtyard. This nursing sister held onto her starched rigid triangular veil at the top of her head, worried that the hair grips would not be enough to prevent it flying off. She was stooped into the wind, but Scott could see her scarlet tippet and her QARANC medal bouncing against her right breast with each breathless step she took, her shiny black shoes gripped tight to the shingle gravel stoned surface. He could see that under her grey dress she wore brown hosiery. 'Oh,' exclaimed Scott, squinting into the mirror to take in the sight of her, now getting used to seeing ghosts as if they were an everyday occurrence, 'I always thought they wore light grey stockings or tights.'

'Yes they did Scott, but years later, it was American Tan colours during the 1950s and 1960 when the QAs became a Corps on 1st February 1949. Their uniform changed soon after. Before that it was black hosiery.'

'Oh. So, she haunts this place? Wait a minute,' cried out Scott, 'you're still here, you haven't disappeared despite glowing orange and using your energy.'

'No, that's because she's not a ghost, just a small memory from this place, a bit like when the Grey Lady took you to the Battle of Loos. Though she knew how to do it on a larger scale. This small memory doesn't zap my energy, nor did showing you the theatre ghosts back in Aberdeen.'

Scott quickly twigged, 'So you can take me back in time to any military event, say like The Falklands War?'

Naomi sighed, 'yes, though I might come to regret letting you know that, you're going to have me whizzing you here, there and everywhere, studying various battles.'

'Ohhh,' replied Scott, like a child entering a well-stocked sweet shop with coins burning a hole in his pocket.

'Oh dear, what have I started!' exclaimed Naomi. 'Of course though the nursing sister was not a ghost, it doesn't mean that Tedworth House is without its ghosts,' warned Naomi.

Chapter 19

'Anyway, enough procrastinating Scott, it's time you went to see him. Besides, anyone looking out of a window or walking past will wonder why you are taking to an empty passenger seat.'

'I know, I know, but what do I say, it's been over three years.'

'Don't worry Scott, he won't have been sat there waiting for you to visit, he's been busy too. Besides, you two always got on well, now off you go,' she chided, shooing her hands towards him in an effort to hurry him along, they had much to do.

'And you'll be with me?'

'Every step of the way, haggis muncher, now get going.' She felt like a mum chasing her errant child off to the first day of school after the long summer break.

Scott eased himself out of the car, feeling a bit stiff after the nine-hour journey. He crunched along the gravel path and used the ramp to enter the building. He looked behind him to see if Naomi was following, she wasn't. Instead she was now by his side when he returned his glance. He was just in time to see her mischievously walk through the shut door. She stopped so that she was half in and half out and gave him a conspiratorial wave. He'd only just now had time to think about what she said, something about the old Mansion House not being without ghosts. Was that really why they were here? He

149

dismissed the thought as quickly as it entered his head. Who cared, so long as they were together. He quickened his step and found himself in a palatial entrance hall with ornate plastered ceilings, the intricate embellishments above stood out in sharp contrast to the modern day art work adorning the walls and the plush leather sofas and armchairs around the wooden flooring. There, sat laughing at the comical adventures of Oor Wullie from an old copy of The Sunday Post, was their friend. Naomi had already tried wrapping her arms around him, giving off her warming orange glow to show her pleasure.

'Scott,' he shouted across the cavernous entrance hall, 'good tae see you loon.'

Scott walked across with his arm outstretched, ready to shake his hand, but Billie ignored that and went straight to the man hug, with none of the awkward shoulder bumping: it was a full on warm embrace of kinship, of brothers in arms reunited after a tough battle. Their war had been Afghanistan and the last time either had set eyes on the other was in the back of a Chinook. This was the helicopter in which Scott was supposed to be the heroic rescuer, but he had ended up being rescued by his own colleagues instead. Not that Billie had witnessed much of this, he was heavily sedated and the last time Scott had seen him he was going into cardiac arrest. He still felt guilty that his thoughts were not on saving him, but on reaching his beloved Naomi. If only Billie could see her now, wrapping her arms around them both in an attempt at a group hug.

'How you been man, glad you could make it, you here for long?'

'I'm good Billie, really good, though feeling a bit squashed.'

Billie laughed, 'sorry mate, a'body tells me that I've become a tree hugger since my injury, but man I'm glad to be alive.' He released Scott from the embrace, but continued to hold him by the shoulders, 'it's great to see you laddie. Come sit down, were the roads clear?' He finally released his grip on Scott and motioned to the deep sofa. They sat down together.

'Aye, nae bad, the usual traffic at Birmingham, the sat nav took me through the M6 Toll.'

'Ouch,' sympathised Billie, 'how much did you get stung for?'

'£5-50 would you believe!'

'Man, and they call us Scots tight! So how long are you here for,' asked Billie, repeating his earlier question.

'Just a few nights, I'm teaching the 1st Battalion The Royal Welsh Fusiliers and others of the Lead Armoured Infantry Task Force how to administer effectively the new lozenge painkiller. It'll be standard issue by next year.'

'Oh, aye,' said Billie, 'a lollipop in the battlefield, fitever next. So you all ready to sing Men of Harlech with them tomorrow? Brave lads though, Operation Moshtarak was tough for them.'

Scott laughed, 'not quite, I haven't a male Welsh choir voice; I'd sound more like a screaming banshee. But I'm getting out and about over the next few months, so I'll probably know most of the British Army songs and marches by then. So how's the leg?'

'Ach, nae bad, though the Taliban shot out most of my thigh muscle, I've still got nerve damage, it drags a bit when I walk. Running's out of the question, I've had numerous physiotherapy sessions and am still desk bound. I guess I'm one of the lucky ones though when I think of what happened to the rest of the lads and your poor Naomi.'

'Aye,' Scott agreed, though if only you could see her, sat next to you, looking ever so happy to see you. 'So 4 Scots have kept you on then?'

'Aye, but not for long. I miss real soldiering, not shuffling bits of paper around.' He raised his left hand in the air and twiddled around his silver Celtic ring, 'Fiona and I got wed two years ago, we missed you at the wedding, but your dad did write a lovely letter explaining how ill you were. You took a fair knock.'

'Without firing a shot in anger, I feel a bit of a fraud sometimes.'

'Nonsense, a team medic and nurse out in the streets of Iraq; that took some nerve.'

'Maybe,' said a reluctant Scott. 'So what brings you here?'

'That's me out of the army now Scott, one final round of physio-terrorism and I'm off to civvy street. I get to lark about on the Skiplex tomorrow whilst you teach the Welsh lads to suck lollipops!'

'Sounds like you've got the better bargain,' replied Scott feeling envious that Billie would spend the day indoor skiing whilst he tried to make his thick broad Aberdonian accent understood by a room full of Welsh lads and lassies.

'What about you though, have you done anything exciting since Afghanistan?'

'Recover mostly. It took some time to get over the head injury. I had lots of physiotherapy but soon got back to work. I was part of the team that took the rapid response field hospital out on its first exercise. Well really it was to show to a group of VIPs from other armies. All the same, it was good to put the vanguard hospital through its paces.'

'That's the one that fits into two C17 transporter planes?' questioned Billie.

'Aye, that's the one. About 100 wire cargo cages and us lot. It's brilliant, we can fly off anywhere, land, and then be up and running within about sixteen hours. The RAMC CMTs are fantastic at putting up the trusty green canvas tents. We all chip in, even the top surgeons and anaesthetists. It's the combat medical technicians who are the real experts at putting together the wards and operating theatre though. They start with the operating theatre because that's always needed first. We can treat eight soldiers straight away. We even take an ambulance with us. The whole thing provides as good a care, maybe even better, though I'm biased, than an NHS trauma centre.'

'Sounds great man, I know I'm going to miss the army. I've been told to expect a longer waiting period at National Health Service hospitals, even though we've got that covenant. What about x-ray machines and scanners, you surely can't take all those big machines?'

'Yes we do Billie, state of the art stuff too, affa pricey. The radiographers use a wheeled x-ray machine called the Dragon, it looks a bit like the robot in the film Short Circuit.

'Number Five is alive!' quoted Billie.

'That's the mannie! There's even an intensive care ward with all the gadgets. Someone once counted two hundred and fifty bits of electrical equipment that goes beep. That keeps the Royal Engineer sparkies busy with the generators. They have to make sure all two hundred and sixty eight plug sockets work, as well as the six air-conditioning units and the eighty six lights. Our record so far is eleven hours to set up, but it did need one hundred of us working flat out. We couldn't manage that in the desert heat mind.'

'No, the heat in The Stan was something, the desert is even worse,' agreed Billie.

'Aye, we were at Al-Quwayrah in Jordan; affa hot there mate. The trick is in the planning,' confided Scott. 'We pack the planes so that the gear we want first is packed last, so there is no messing around. It's tents off first and we all work as a team erecting them before going off to the various departments and wards. We can work in most spaces, and once fully built it takes up fifty square metres. I worked in the ward where there were twelve beds during the exercise, I'm hoping to work in the two bedded emergency bay next time.'

'So it really is a hospital in a box then Scott?'

'Ha, aye, a'body keeps calling it that.'

'So do you all stay there, wherever you land?'

'Not always, it depends on the casualties needs, we treat and stabilise and can get our wounded troops back to Birmingham usually within twenty-four hours if needed. We can take about one hundred and sixty units of blood in a special fridge.'

Billie involuntary rubbed his tattoo on his upper arm that declared his blood group under a St. Andrews flag.

'You still into military history?' asked Billie.

Scott ignored Naomi who was feigning slapping her hand on her forehead as if to say, 'what a stupid question,' or 'don't get him started.'

'Aye, why.'

'Ah, then let me tell you who used this as a residence during the First World War, only General Sir Charles Douglas. He was the General Officer Commander-in-Chief of Southern Command, and one of us.'

'You mean a fellow Scot?'

''Aye, but better than that,' continued Billie, 'he was a fellow Gordon Highlander.'

'He did well for himself then, some rank to get to,' marvelled Scott.

'Aye and he had a connection with us two.'

'Really?' asked Scot.

'Aye, he fought in the 1879 Afghan War. He was mentioned in despatches twice and took part in the march from Kabul for the relief of Kandahar. I read it in a book about the history of this place. Imagine that; fighting in the Stan more than a century before us. He then went on to fight in the South African War of 1881 and the Sudan Campaign four years later. As if that wasn't enough he then fought in the Boer War. Quite the soldier.'

Scott whistled at this, 'Nae wonder they made him a General.'

'He met a sad end though. He was the last person to use this building as a private house and went on to become the personal assistant to the King. Just as he took up this prestigious office, he died, a few months after the Great War started. I think the building then became an officer's club. I bet they'd twirl furiously in their graves if they saw the likes of me sat here in their Mess! It's a Grade II listed building now.'

'Poor chap, what a career though.'

'Talking of graves, I'll have to tell you about the ghost!'

'Oh aye?' said Scott, wondering why he keeps attracting talk of or seeing ghosts.

'Some nonsense about bangs in the middle of the night, been happening for decades apparently. I heard them the other night, I reckon it's just the old water pipes, the heating system is really old here.'

The two sat in companionable silence for a moment or two before Scott glanced up at the clock on the wall. 'Is that the time! I'm supposed to have checked into the transit block at the barracks. I'd better get a move on. Can I meet you later for a drink Billie?'

'Aye, that sounds good, how about going to the British Legion Club, I ken most folk think that it's full of old men, but the beer is really cheap, just don't tell Fiona, she thinks I don't drink whilst taking these new tablets for my pain. It helps me get to sleep, ye ken?'

Scott laughed and prepared himself for another rib breaking man hug. Billie didn't disappoint.

As Scott made his way back to the car he caught Naomi looking up to one of the tall windows on the first floor. He assumed it must have been Billie's room. He was unaware of being watched by a pale thin figure, dressed in grey. She had her mouth wide open, as if in mid scream.

Chapter 20

'What caught your eye Naomi?' asked Scott, now back in his car. She was once more by his side, but looking puzzled.

'Oh, nothing really, just admiring the building, I kind of get your interest in old military buildings now.'

'They don't make them like that anymore,' they said in unison, though only Scott was laughing.

Quickly changing the subject Naomi asked, 'would you mind if we had a change in music, I've missed Radio 2. We're a bit late for Steve Wright in the Afternoon, but let's see what else is on.'

Scott obliged and reluctantly ejected his favourite CD and pushed the button that auto-tuned to the correct station and was greeted by the deep rasping welcoming voice of Bob Harris and his Country show. He was announcing the next song as an up and coming musician from Aberdeenshire by the name of Colin Clyne. Scott chortled, 'the loon fae Stonehaven is doing michty fine!'

Naomi tutted, as Doin' Fine was played in the car once more, 'well, at least you've stopped sulking,' she said belligerently, though her foot was moving away to the rhythmic melody of Colin strumming away on his guitar as he belted out his heart-felt song.

Scott continued to laugh to himself as he popped in the Postcode to Lucknow Barracks, and then his laughter subsided, 'oh, you were right, it's just down the road.'

'Of course it is, you numptee, they wouldn't have made the nursing sisters walk too far to work, would they. Not many people could afford cars in 1929, when they first moved into Tedworth House.'

Scott turned off his sat nav and drove them 'down the road'. He pulled up to the standard red topped and white gate barrier and showed his MOD 90 identity card to the combat-uniformed soldier guard who was carrying his L85A2 version of the SA80 rifle at the ready. 'Alright mate, I'm Corporal Scott Grey, I should be booked in to teach your lads and lassies how to use the new painkiller fentanyl lozenge.'

The soldier gave Scott a nod to wait and mouthed something into his Personal Role Radio, the four metre walk to the guardroom being too far from him, though of course he couldn't leave his important post. Scott could see the duty Corporal flicking slowly through a sheaf of paper on a clipboard before giving the guard a thumbs up through the window.

'Okay Scott, nice to meet you, I'm Gareth, I'm afraid you can't take your car beyond this point, but there is a huge car park to your left,' he helpfully pointed and continued, 'you can leave your kit here though to save you carrying it. Have you heavy gear?'

Scott couldn't help himself, 'just a bag of lollipops.' He said to the confused looking guard.

Chapter 21

Scott slung his rucksack over his shoulder, shut the boot and locked his car. He then returned the short distance to the guardroom. 'Hello again Gareth, where should I go then?'

Gareth pointed across the parade-ground to an old red-bricked building with two floors and old fashioned white painted windows that looked single-glazed. 'I'm afraid you're in the transit block Scott, room 3. It's not the most comfortable of places, a bit draughty. I think it used to be an old hospital. Hope it's not haunted!' He handed Scott a key.

Scott grinned, 'sounds ideal! See you later Gareth.'

As he walked around the empty parade ground perimeter he noticed that Naomi was now with him, looking over her left shoulder, a frown crossing her face.

'You okay quine?' asked Scott trying to follow her eye line to see what she was frowning at; 'I did lock the car, didn't I?'

Naomi turned back to Scott, 'mmm, yes.' She pointed across to the red-bricked building; 'not the best of digs. But I don't think that's the old hospital, looks more like an old Quartermaster's store.'

'Probably is, you know how rumours start and then continue over the years. Gareth probably heard it from someone who heard it from someone, you know how it is. So where is the old military hospital then?'

'I thought it was at Delhi Barracks, nearby. The old sisters and nurses where I got my information from worked in an isolation, surgical and children's ward.'

'What nurses would these be then?' asked Scott, puzzled.

'On the spiritual plain, that's why I have such a bank of information, we can access each-others knowledge. It's a bit like me now having the Grey Lady's knowledge.'

'Like the Borg collective in Star Trek, but friendlier?' quipped Scott.

'In a way yes,' replied a distant Naomi, once more looking over her shoulder. Scott was too busy looking up at the brickwork surrounding the window; they were of a deeper red shade and looked almost painted. Definitely pre-World War One he thought.

'Ooookkkayy,' wrestled Scott with his thoughts, 'it's all a bit freaky this, but who cares! I'll go with the flow.' He smiled at her lovingly as together they walked towards the steps of the building and entered.

Scott slung his rucksack onto the green plastic covered mattress. He wondered where the bedding was.

Naomi was looking around, 'well it might have been part of the hospital, the corridor outside could have been part of the Nightingale ward design, especially as the bathrooms are at the end. Builders could easily have sectioned off these rooms. But I always thought that Delhi Barracks was where the old Tidworth Military Hospital was. One of the nurses spoke about nursing in a Delhi Hut and caring for patients who had just had operations. It was separated from the main wing of the hospital and looked just like a hutted building out in the Raj. It even had an open balcony and was built on stilts, as if to keep rats and bugs out like they do in the tropics. The nursing staff used to joke that the architect must have got the plans wrong and that somewhere out in India there would be a bricked ward built to shelter from snow, ice, wind and rain. The patients there must have been boiling! Did you know they had to wheel their patients from here to the operating theatre by going outside?'

'Never,' said a disbelieving Scott. 'That wouldn't have been practical on a rainy day.'

'No really, the operating theatre was also on the other side of the building, so they'd have to use umbrellas and waterproof clothing to shelter their patients as they trundled them along on trolleys under a flimsy awning walkway. The orthopaedic ward patients fared better, they were in the main hospital, on the ground floor.'

Scott looked at her, not sure whether to believe her or not.

'But then again I'm almost certain that the hospital was red-bricked like this one.'

'This one would fit in with the era; the red lintel above the windows is of a type of brick favoured by builders back then. Did you see how shiny it still looks, almost like new.'

Naomi continued to look down the corridor, still lost in thought as she said, 'you're also teaching the 1st Armoured Infantry Brigade whilst you are here, aren't you?'

'Aye, in two days' time, over at Delhi Barracks, I'll just walk there; it'll save problems with parking.'

'It may well have been knocked down and not retained like the Old Royal Herbert Military Hospital in Woolwich, which are now luxury flats for top earning Londoners. Anyway let's have a look around Delhi Barracks whilst you are there and see. Talking of which, I want to satisfy my curiosity and see if the bathrooms look like old military hospital toilets and baths. I'm still not sure if this is the old army hospital that closed in 1977. I'll just look down there.'

'Fine lass, I need to make my bed, if I can find sheets.'

'I'll leave you with a piece of trivia Scott; I know how much you like hearing it. James Blunt, the singer, was born at Tidworth Military Hospital.'

'You're beautiful, You're beautiful, You're beautiful, it's true,' sang Scott.

Naomi smiled, but upon turning to walk down the long corridor, her orange hue, turned to a dull red as she walked further away, unnoticed by the still singing Scott.

He was looking across to the built-in white wardrobes, 'that'll be where the sheets are,' he said to himself, interrupting his song, not realising he was alone.

He walked across to open them and jumped back, his blood turned to ice, making him immobile. All he wanted to do was run away, but he was frozen to the spot at this new sight. He felt that tightening around his stomach and testes as fear gripped his bowels and terror flooded his body. There, squatting in the wardrobe, below the shelves that held the bedding, was a wild haired woman in a dirt-ridden tattered grey dress. She was bare footed and her feet, legs and arms were streaked with dried blood and earth. She was rocking back in forth as best she could in the confines of the wardrobe, mumbling incoherently. Her neck suddenly turned to Scott with a loud crack like that of a branch snapping from a tree during a tempestuous storm. Her mouth opened and worms flooded out along with clods of earth. They tumbled and slithered towards the still petrified Scott. They were joined by multitudes of spiders that squeezed through gaps in the floorboards by his shoes. They quickly crawled and thronged with the worms to be the first to climb up his legs just as she finally found her voice and screamed out 'HELP ME!!!!' Wide eyed she now jumped from the wardrobe in one bound and came face to face with Scott, her breath a noxious cloud of green hazy putrification that billowed around him. She looked straight into his eyes, her neck bowing from side to side like a swaying ship near rocks in a violent sea. With a demented whirl she brought up her hands to Scott's lips, her long, filthy nails just touching the tip of his nose, which felt to him as sharp scratches.

She then lowered them frantically and reached into Scott's chest, her forearm disappearing as if stretching through into his soul for what she wanted. Her scream pierced the air as if the hounds of hell were chasing her and with one final cloud of gas she vanished through Scott, leaving no trace of her presence other than the ashen look on his face and the trembling that coursed through his body as feeling was once more returned to him. He fell sideward against the bed, eyes shut; reminiscent of his fall on the helicopter, only this time he was alone with no-one to save him.

Chapter 22

Rubidub dum, rubidub dum went the drummer boy, furiously with his drumsticks as they lashed against the stretched and tightened hide of his drum. He was commanding attention, demanding he be heard above all else, knowing that his time for action had come. Like on the battlefield, in death he would direct and order. Rubidub dum, rubidub dum, rubidub dum, rubidub dum echoed around and repeated as if bouncing acoustically around an empty building. Only this echo grew louder and louder with each violent beat, threatening to shatter all that stood in its way. His time had come again, and he would, must, listen and act. His pounding became louder, unbearable, insistent. Rubidub dum, rubidub dum, rubidub dum, rubidub dum…

Chapter 23

Rubidub dum, rubidub dum, rubidub dum, rubidub dum, whirled and rejoiced with its near triumph around Scott's head. He was oblivious to all else but this sound as he lay sprawled over his rucksack, part on and part off the mattress. His eyes, though shut, were moving rapidly beneath his eyelids, as if in the deepest of REM sleep. Only this rapid eye movement was from the darkest nightmare, the most disturbing of visions: the actualisation that she was a reality; and that she had reached into his very soul and found him wanting. It disturbed him and penetrated his unconscious mind.

Chapter 24

His phone vibrated in his back pocket; tingling his skin as the ringtone pierced deep into his mind, still unaware of what he'd experienced, still struggling to come to terms with this latest ghostly encounter. His body had shut down, to protect him, to envelope him in safety. But he battled through the vanishing green fog and opened his eyes to see something, no someone, who could and would always save him. His Naomi.

'You've finally met her then Scott? She's now shown herself to you.'

He could hear her speak. He could still hear the plaintive ringtone just as it stopped and went to voicemail. But it was all so distant, as if they were from another room and he was able to hear a stranger's one-sided conversation through thin walls. He heard his Sergeant's voice again, the one from when he was a young recruit, 'up and at 'em boy.'

Only this time he would not obey. He closed his eyes in defiance. He'd just lie here a bit longer, thank you very much. Let Morpheus, the Greek God of Dreams care for him a bit longer. He needed the restorative power of sleep.

'Wake up Scott!' shouted Naomi, 'we have much to do.'

Rubidub dum, rubidub dum, rubidub dum, rubidub dum, echoed around his mind, but duller, not as sharp, not as demanding. It slowly became less intense, gradually fading away to a nothingness, until he finally woke up to the lovelier sight of Naomi bending down over him, wearing that dress, the one she wore to engagement party, all sparkly and blue, curvaceous and clinging, like a second skin. He smiled, who cares if this was another memory, he'd stay with this one, thank you very much again. He sighed blissfully, almost post-coitally; here was another of his happy places and times.

'Sorry Scott, can't have you sleeping on the job,' she again shouted, as she rubbed her hands together and a whirlwind powered up from her amber glow until it was ablaze and arced out of her and into Scott. He leapt up with a sharp inhalation of breath that warmed him to the core and heightened his senses. He could feel it infusing down his throat, one half coursing through his lungs and bloodstream, the other flushing through his bowels, purging the earthen intrusion away like the after-taste of a peaty malt whisky. 'What the f...!' What was that, who was she, what did you just do…?

'Steady Scott, take your time, stand up when you are ready. You may feel giddy for a bit longer, until the purge finishes. That, I'm afraid, is why we are here. She followed us from the old nursing quarters. For decades the nurses thought that she was one of theirs, a dead QA haunting their bedrooms. Only she wasn't. They would catch glimpses of her in their mirrors as the glass tried to capture her soul. They would just see a swoosh of grey pass them by in the reflection. But it was not the grey of a nursing uniform they saw. It was something less pleasant.'

'She, she looked like a vagrant, someone sleeping rough in the woods,' said Scott, slowly rising from his rucksack pillow.

'Yes, for centuries she did,'

'No way, no-one lives that long.'

'She's not alive Scott, coaxed Naomi, waiting for Scott to work it out for himself, needing him to do so.

'That's why you kept looking over your shoulder, you saw her at the window at Tedworth House?'

'Yes Scott, her spirit followed us here, she died in the woods nearby, two centuries ago. She latched onto my spiritual energy. I'm so sorry, I had not realised just how powerful she had become. Her need is great and growing. But she is gone, for now, you are safe. Sorry I left you, I wanted so much for this to be the old military hospital, but looking around; I really don't think it is.'

'So what does she want,' questioned Scott, now on his feet, dusting down his clothes as if trying to eradicate the woman's presence physically.

'I think I know, but it is so important for you to have faith, not just in God, but in yourself.'

'You mean you want me to work this one out for myself, like a test?'

'If you like Scott, it is more of me wanting you to have the confidence in your gift from The Grey Lady though.' Naomi looked worried, but ploughed on, he had to know. 'One day, soon, we are going to be tested together, not like this, but in casting out great evil, a wicked man. I need you to be fighting fit Scott. Remember what other kinder ghosts have told you; some will not go easily.'

Scott, despite his ordeal, laughed. He flexed his muscles in the classic body builder pose, but without all the daft spray tan. 'I've had months of work in the gym.'

'Ha, ha,' laughed Naomi, glad to have the old Scott back, 'and you look great for it, but I mean mentally fighting fit, and spiritually.'

Scott looked to his shoes, not just to check that the spiders and worms weren't still lurking, but also remembering why he'd lost his faith, twice in his life. So much death, so much loss he thought. I miss them both, even if I do have one back, it's not the same. I so want to hold her, make love with her, he thought. 'Not yet, I try, but not yet. I still can't comprehend why a loving God, if there is a God, would take mum and you from me.'

'But he brought me back to you Scott, it was predestined and…'

Scott interrupted her, '… and God works in mysterious ways. Well what I saw was certainly mysterious. Okay, I'll try.' Remembering his phone call, he reached into his back pocket and dialled the number for his voice mail. He put it up to his ear and said, 'that was Billie, he'll meet me at the Legion at 8. He's got to go to a safety briefing about the Skiplex tonight. That gives us time to check out Delhi Barracks.'

'No Scott, you need to rest, that encounter has shaken you up more than you think. Why don't you go early to the British Legion Club, you'll get a nice surprise there.

Chapter 25

Scott looked up to the metal archway with the signage that proudly announced "Royal British Legion" in large gold lettering. Beyond was a straight path that led to a single-storied building. He shivered, remembering some of the dreams he had experienced in his flat in Aldershot, just before his encounter with the Grey Lady. They were all so vivid, but this is one of the ones that haunted him the most; because he knew why. It was the unimaginable horrors contained within, the ovens, the piles of rotten corpses and the decaying bodies left to decompose all around the camp. The archway signage made him think of "Arbeit Macht Frel" three small German words that had him crying and screaming into the dark on many a night. Thank heavens that little Thomas and his mum Wendy could not hear him through their thick shared walls in the flat next door. The phrase translated to "Work sets you free" and they were above the entrances to many Concentration Camps, such as Auschwitz, run by the Nazis and their fervently evil SS Officers. But Bergen-Belsen was the one of his nightmares. Please God don't take me back in time to then, he wasn't mentally tough enough to face those horrors, not yet anyway, he thought.

He turned to Naomi, who was once more walking beside him. He said angrily, 'surely this can't be the nice surprise, reminding me of my nightmares?'

'Have faith in me Scott,' she said patiently. 'Know that I will always love you, and will not see harm done to you.'

'Mmm,' said a sceptical Scott, 'except for what happened back in that room.'

'And I've said sorry, but I also know just how strong you are, mentally.'

'So why do I still yell out at these nightmares and greet like a bairn when I wake up?'

'Even the toughest man, or woman would Scott. That's why you were given this Gift, because you can cope, and will go on coping,' she continued gently. 'Now go up this path, enter those doors and get your surprise!'

'Mmm,' said a doubtful Scott, 'okay.'

As he entered the bar area he eyed the ubiquitous rows of plaques from various regiments and corps of the army, squadrons of the Royal Air Force and crests of the ships and bases of the Royal Navy. You could walk into any Legion throughout the UK and feel right at home, he thought. He smiled as he heard the booming Yorkshire voice deep in conversation with an elderly gentleman across the room at one of the tables. His smile spread wider across his face, now this was a proper surprise. He approached the bar, 'Hello lass, could I please have an Appletiser with no ice, and the same again for those two chaps, I'm betting that one of them is a pint of bitter.'

'Well, yes, it is; do you know him then?'

'Aye and right glad I am too. Please take one for yourself and could you please pop them on a tray along with three different flavoured packets of crisps, I know how hungry he gets.'

'Ha ha, that he does, he'd eat us out of house and home that one, given half the chance,' she said as she expertly pumped away to pour the pint of bitter.

Scott looked around the optics, he did miss being able to have a wee dram, but his medicines took first priority. He wondered if he should go into nurse mode and talk to Billie about the risks of drinking alcohol whilst taking strong painkillers. He thought better of it, remembering how much bigger than him he was, his ribs were still sore from the man hug! He spotted some Pork Scratching and Scampi Fries packets poking out amongst the choice of spirits, 'could we also have two packets of each of those please lass, thanks.'

Naomi sat down on one of the bar stools next to Scott, a smug look on her face, as if to say 'see, trust me!'

Scott winked at her whilst the barmaid had her back to him, picking out different flavours. This really was a timely present; he hadn't seen him for about a year, their duties always clashing.

'That'll be £18-50 please love.'

'Cheers lass, could you please put the change in the poppy tin, thanks,' said Scott handing over a Scottish twenty-pound note, glad that the barmaid wasn't one of those that still refused to accept guid Scots currency. He picked up the tray and ambled over, careful not to spill any of the well poured pints.

'Mind if I join you gentleman? Like the three wise men, I come bearing gifts!' He squeezed the tray onto the table, careful not to knock their almost empty glasses over.

The big burly man ruffled his unruly hair, 'Well bless me, if it isn't Scott, how are you my boy, you look it great shape,' said Padre Caldwell, answering his own question. 'Good Lord above, you've brought enough snacks to feed the five thousand all over again. It's great to see you,' he boomed, 'what brings you to this neck of the woods?'

Scott resisted saying 'lollipops' least this sweet-toothed army chaplain seek some from him. Instead, as he took his jacket off and rummaged around in his pocket he replied, 'I'm training some of the local regiments in the new battlefield first aid treatments. Ahh ha, I knew I had some.' He placed a white and blue packet onto the table, by the padre.

'Come and sit down my dear boy, this is Harold, Harold meet Scott, one of our caring army nurses. We go back all the way to Iraq and Afghanistan, I follow him about like a bad penny,' said the padre, giving a deep rumbling laugh at his own joke.

Scott reached his hand across to Harold, judging rightly that this 60 something year old veteran would be more comfortable with a handshake, rather than a fist bump or man hug. 'Pleased to meet you Harold, hope I'm not interrupting?'

'Not at all young man, always pleased to make new friends,' he replied as he grasped Scott's hand, 'I was just about to tell the padre here about our ghost.'

'Oh,' replied Scott, who was thinking 'Geez oh, how many more do I have to see this week?'

'Don't worry son, it's not in this building,' he gave a furtive look around him, 'at least I don't think so!'

The padre boomed his infectious laugh again. 'Go on Harold, I can't resist a good ghost story, Scott's told me a few about the old army hospital ghosts in Germany in the past. He'll love to hear it too.'

'Aye, I will, but first get your lips around these pints lads whilst I return the empties.' Scott waited until both men drained the remains of their first pint and gratefully helped themselves to the free drinks, crisps and snacks.

He quickly returned the tray and empty glasses to the bar and gave the barmaid a big thumbs up. She was busy chatting to her next customer and pouring another pint, but gave him a cheeky wink. He was glad that Naomi didn't see the wink: she was too busy trying to wrap her arms around the considerable girth of the padre whilst hugging onto his shoulder. He returned to them, pulling up a fourth chair. 'I've a friend coming at eight, hope you don't mind?'

'Not all all,' said both men in unison, Harold was secretly hoping for another free drink from another new friend.

'So what's this ghost then?' enquired Scott of Harold whilst discretely watching Naomi take the seat intended for Billie. He hoped she wouldn't mind that he would have to ignore her, least the two men thought he was crackers talking to an empty seat.

'It's well known in Tidworth and dates back to March 1661.' He took a slurp of his pint, as if preparing his lips for lots of thirsty tall tale telling, 'mighty kind of you to buy a round and some snacks, thanks so much.'

'Harold here is ex Royal Electrical and Mechanical Engineers,' explained the padre, reaching over for the blue and white packet. 'Ahhh, pandrops, lovely Scott, thank you, I love these, can't get them down here in England.' He opened the packet and popped one of the thick cylindrical mint sweets from Scotland into his mouth and noisily started sucking away. He pushed them towards Harold.

'And a great time I had too, us REME chaps got everywhere, repairing all sorts of equipment. I even found myself at Tidworth Military Hospital on several occasions, odd building set up.'

Scott made a mental note to ask him later how to find the building.

Harold continued, 'Anyway, getting back to the ghost story, it happened soon after a fellow called William Drury was arrested. He claimed to be a military drummer under Cromwell who had fallen on hard times and would beg on the streets by playing his drum. He was basically a vagrant chancing his luck and begging unlicensed in the street. He would demand money from people whilst beating out a military tune. It was common practice then to award English Civil War soldiers a licence to beg. These permits gave them a means to make money from village to village as they made their way home. Only William didn't have a permit. Others say he was using a fraudulent license. So the local Magistrate,

John Mompesson, confiscated his drum to stop him making a nuisance of himself in the nearby village of Ludgershall and charged him for causing an affray. I don't know why, but the magistrate took it upon himself to get the bailiff to fetch the drum and have it brought to his house. I think he lived in Zouch Manor, though, of course, the village was known as Tedworth in those days, not Tidworth. But the house is now named locally as Mompesson House. Then the magistrate had to go away from home on some business and Mrs Mompesson was in the house with her two daughters, the mother-in-law and some servants, and that's when some odd noises started.'

'What sort of odd noises?' asked the padre, making some of his own now that he was tucking into the Pork Scratchings.

'It started as banging on the walls from the children's room, and then sinister scratchings from under the bed,' Harold explained.

Scott shuddered, remembering the demented woman's long dirty fingernails clawing at his nostrils.

'But that's not the worst of it, the children were then lifted up into the air and a used chamber pot was tipped onto the bed.'

'Like poltergeist activity,' contributed the padre between munches.

'That's right padre, and it went on for two years. People blamed it on William Drury as punishment for taking his drum from him. But by this time he was in prison in Gloucester for thieving. When asked by folks, he would always say; "Aye, I have plagued him and he shall never be quiet till he hath made me satisfaction for taking away my drum." Well, that got him tried as a witch at Salisbury and he was sentenced to transportation. During that time the phenomena stopped and things settled down for the magistrate and his family.'

'But...' encouraged Scott as he sat forward.

'Yes, there's always a but, isn't there! The noises came back when he returned to Britain, the sailors said he commanded the frightening storms that lashed their ship and they were unable to complete their voyage. News of these events reached London and a Royal Commission inquiry was set up by King Charles II no less. He sent Lord Falmouth and Lord Chesterfield to investigate, but nothing happened. So Sir Christopher Wren was sent and he noticed that the sounds only happened when certain maid-servants were in the next room. He noted that the walls were thin boards. Others said it was done deliberately by all the servants to scare the unpopular mother. One servant claimed she saw a body with red and glaring eyes. But yet the noises continued and all sorts have been blamed, including gypsies who cursed the magistrate for confiscating the drum and imprisoning the drummer. Others noted that the thumpings were coming from the external walls and the roof. So,' he looked to the padre, 'a minister of the church was called, Mr Cragge his name was. He offered up prayers and felt a bed staffe thrown against his legs whilst saying them.'

The padre nodded knowingly, as if he was acknowledging his own experience of the supernatural.

Harold continued, 'even the children's legs got hit and they turned black and blue. Visitors to the house reported their money in their pockets turning black and the couple told of a long spike found in his old mother's bed. The house almost became a tourist spot and a group of men decided, whilst William was in jail again, to shout out "Satan, if the drummer set thee to work, give three knocks, and no more" and…' Harold paused for effect and to take a sip of his free pint.

'And…' asked Scott, now on the edge of his seat.

'There were three distinct knocks, one clearly after the other; and no more than three. So they, which included Sir Thomas Chamberlain of Oxford, asked that if it was the Drummer then it should give five knocks, and five were heard. Well that sealed William's fate. Oh, wait a minute; I think that I may have gotten that bit out a bit too late because these events are why he was tried as a witch. I think I've told the story correctly, maybe just in the wrong date order. But that's the story of what is now known as the Tedworth demon drummer. It was even turned into a play by the essayist Joseph Addison in 1715. He was the chap who started The Spectator magazine in 1711. His play went by the titles The Drummer or The Haunted House, depending on where it was being held.'

Harold turned back to the padre again and continued, 'and another Reverend, Joseph Glanvill, wrote a treatise called Saducismus Triumphatus 'Saduceism Defeated' in which he defended witchcraft and the supernatural. Many famous ghost hunters, like Harry Price and Alan Gauld, quoted from it.'

'There are more things in heaven and earth, Horatio,' quoted the Padre.

'Well, yes Padre, for in the 1950s the then owner of the house, Denis Martineau received a visit from a Mr Hammick and he told him the tale of this drummer. Denis then fetched a brass badge that he found under the floorboards of the room in which the drum was said to have been locked in. It was a drummer's brass badge. Now the noises are heard in the library, where the badge is kept; no-one knows where the drum is now, well no-one alive anyway.'

'So, where's this house then?' asked Scott.

'It's the farmhouse-looking building close to the old Norman Church of the Holy Trinity, let your nose guide you.' said Harold cryptically.

'Eh,' said a puzzled Scott.

'You can smell a vile sulphurous odour. It gets stronger the nearer you get. The Council have had the drains up so many times, but the smell continues.'

Scott wondered if they smelt worse than the woman who had attacked him earlier. He was just wondering if there was a connection when he spotted Billie and gave him a welcoming wave. Naomi moved to stand by Padre Caldwell in anticipation of Billie joining them.

'It's closed now, but my lads from the unit used to drink at the Drummer Pub, just off Station Road, because that's where the hospital staff drank. Some of them met their spouses there.' Harold started rhythmically banging the table. Rubidub dum, rubidub dum he tapped out, over and over again.

Scott turned around at this noise and went pale, 'what's that noise you're tapping?' he asked of Harold.

'Why, the tune of the Tidworth demon drummer of course.'

'That's the noises you hear in your head, isn't it Scott?' asked Naomi, who already knew the answer. They were now back at the transit block accommodation; Scott having bid fond farewells to Padre Caldwell and his new friend Harold. He had also dropped off an inebriated Billie back at Tedworth House. Scott had diligently made sure his friend was safely tucked up in bed. Mischievous Naomi had used some of her spiritual power to momentarily manifest herself to him, gave him a cheeky wink, and rapidly disappeared again. She was still laughing at how Billie had turned to Scott and gibbered that he was never going to mix alcohol and painkillers again. That'll save Scott the dilemma of giving him a lecture she merrily thought!

'Yes, the exact same noises, I've been dying to tell you, this talking to each other without others seeing us is proving difficult, to say the least,' said Scott as he unlocked his room door.

'You could revoke the no bathroom rule, Mr shy! Lots of private time there.'

'A bloke's got to have some privacy lass,' he replied as he stepped tentatively into the room, looking around for the ghostly woman. 'But seriously, it's a bit unnerving that Harold was tapping the exact rhythm out onto the table. That's the first time that anyone else has heard what I've been hearing in my head for months. Do you think I'm being haunted by this William Drury, the Tedworth demon drummer? And why haven't I seen him yet, why hasn't he shown himself?' He was now cautiously opening the wardrobe door, relieved that it only contained two bed sheets, pillows and pillowcases and a dubious looking blanket that looked like it hadn't been washed since the First World War. It was probably issued long before then, he thought. He was glad he always packed a duvet.

Naomi, now standing by the foot of the bed, answered, 'It's definitely a drum being played that you hear, but no, I don't think that you are hearing the Tedworth demon drummer, I don't think he exists. I believe that part in the story that it was maids who were making the noises to torment the magistrate's mother. She wasn't very nice to them and made their lives a misery. No wonder they got their own back on her, though I don't agree with them scaring the two young girls. You still can't see him, can you Scott?' asked Naomi as she gave a kind smile to the space between her and Scott.

'Him?'

'Yes, the person who beats the drum you keep hearing in your head.'

'No, I just get the noises that no-one else seems to hear. They are always there, quietly in the background, like my heartbeat letting me know it's pulsing away. Sometimes they get overwhelming though. And please don't tell me I have to have faith,' replied Scott as he took one of the sheets towards the bed and with the other hand removed his rucksack and put it in the wardrobe. Let's see her get in there with my big gear in the way. He turned back and started to make his bed.

'Okay, faith conversations stop now. But try and recall what you were doing or talking about, or watching on television or hearing on the radio when you heard the worst of the drumming.'

Scott stopped trying to stuff the stained pillow into the pillowcase and turned to Naomi. 'Do you mean that's when he is trying to communicate with me? That the louder it gets, that's when he's trying to talk to me?'

'Yes,' replied Naomi, 'he can't manifest just yet to living beings, something is stopping him…'

'And you're not going to tell me what, because I have to figure it out for myself, as a sign that I am strong enough for this evil man you talked about earlier?'

'Yes Scott.'

'Okay, so I heard them vividly at the Noose and Monkey back in Aberdeen.'

'And why is it called that?' encouraged Naomi.

'Because of some daft story about a monkey dressed like a Frenchman. Sorry I can't see the connection.'

'Think of some other occasions Scott.'

'At the theatre, even Jake, backstage, knew what I was hearing. I still can't see the connection.'

'Yes you can Scott, take some time to think it over. Do something else while you have a think, like unpacking your gear or seeing if the other pillow is a bit cleaner than that one. It looks like too many drunken squaddies have either been sick on it or drooled over a prolonged saucy dream. Gawds!'

'Aye, I think I'll start bringing my own pillows when I go to the next barracks. I'm in Colchester next week.' He started to unpack his stuff from the rucksack, though still kept it in the wardrobe to ensure the strange ghostly woman wouldn't be able to hide there. He felt a bit daft, since she could probably manifest through it, on it or even under it. As he was taking out his iron he thought about the laundry room at the theatre and all the old equipment. The ladies working there in olden days must have worked up a good sweat and probably had toned arm muscles too. Then he remembered, 'the play was about Sergeant Ewart getting an Eagle from the French, so that's a common theme, but I still don't get it.'

Naomi started humming a tune to herself.

'D'oh,' exclaimed Scott, thumping his palm against his forehead. 'Abba was playing on the radio, and the noises were really bad the night dad fell asleep watching the documentary with me. I woke him up by shouting. Fortunately, he thought it was the loud TV. It's Waterloo, isn't it!'

Naomi smiled at him, like a teacher who hears a wayward pupil suddenly answering a difficult question and getting the correct answer.

'They got the lyrics wrong though. Napoleon didn't surrender; he re-mustered, did a tactical retreat and left the battlefield. He wasn't captured that day either. The Allies did find his Imperial coach at Genappe. It still contained his medals and a set of diamonds. The jewels were later used to decorate the Prussian crown jewels. Napoleon abdicated for the second time two days later.'

'You're getting side-tracked Scott,' said Naomi patiently, 'get back to thinking about the connection, you have to solve this in order to move on and get the noises out of your head.'

'And the French had drummer boys, they were there to help the commanders direct the troops, the sounds of their drums and those of the trumpeters would carry over the noise of the battlefield. In those days it was the only way for them to direct a battle.' Scott looked around, 'but I don't see any French drummer boy, and what would he be doing here anyway? Tidworth is a long way from Aberdeen, let alone France.'

'But not from Southampton.'

'Ah,' said Scott, the light dawning in his eyes, 'Ports, but no, I can't recall the French sailing through our harbours.'

'You are so tantalisingly close Scott, why don't you have a shower and get ready for bed, I'm sure you'll work it out after another good night's sleep.'

Scott sniffed his armpits, 'ye still cannae beat the whiff o' an Aberdonian's oxsters quine!' He picked up his towel, shampoo and shower gel and headed off to the shower room.

Steam wafted up the cubicle like rising clouds from a steam engine's chimney whilst cleansing water cascaded down onto Scott, washing away his cares and worries. He wetted his hair and lathered through his shampoo. He closed his eyes and allowed the water pressure to rinse off the lather; he still could not see the French connection. Clear of shampoo, he now opened his eyes so that he could reach out for his shower gel. Instead he stumbled backwards against the cold white tiles at the sight of the raggedy haired woman who was screaming incoherently into his face, right up against his mouth. In the confined space Scott was trapped like a rabbit in a snare. Bits of twigs and leaves fell from her knotted bedraggled hair. They tickled his toes in a menacing way as if tantalising him to try and move further away, knowing that he could not. He could feel her air rush into him like the saving kiss of an exuberant resuscitator as he fought and struggled to flee her grasp, for she had wrapped her filthy arms around his shoulders and was digging in her sharp-taloned fingers almost vice like. Scot winced with pain, trying desperately to release himself from her tight grip, but he could not move his arms. She had caught him like a piece of wood in a vice. He was hers and no Naomi could help him. He felt himself slip amongst his shampoo suds, but he did not fall, such was her grasping control over him. She remained dry despite the hot water rushing down from the shower head. None of her dried blood or mud washed off. Small beetles and cockroaches rushed down out of her eyes as if she were crying tears of insects.

They skittered and ran around his feet, making their way up his legs, to his exposed groin. And still she screamed.

Scott managed to yell out, 'WHAT DO YOU WANT?' and the flow of insects ceased, they disappeared, as if washed away. Her screaming stopped and she looked straight into his eyes, the silence unnerving, the shower water seemed to stop in mid-air. It was as if all of time stood still to allow her the wonder of whether to answer his question, whether it deserved an answer. She released her right arm and her coarse grey dress creaked, as a flow of brown dried muck scattered onto the floor. She cradled his chin and drew him towards him, as if he was a reluctant lover who needed encouragement to kiss. She yelled out 'rubidub dum, rubidub dum,' over and over again.

Chapter 27

She, it, whatever it was, disappeared as quickly as she had come, once again leaving no traces that she had been there. The jet of the shower spurted out a plume of water as it coughed and then cascaded down again, almost like it was clearing its pipes. The twigs, leaves, mud and insects were no longer there, no tell-tale signs lingering in the drain-hole to show that she had been real.

Scott threw open the cubicle's glass door, grabbed his towel and wrapped it around himself as he ran back to his room, slipping on the wet floor on his way to the safety of Naomi. Shampoo and shower gel and all thoughts of washing forgotten. As he turned from the bathroom his bare feet gained a better grip on the carpet, leaving wet indentations behind him. He burst through his door.

'That was quick, has it come to you now?' asked Naomi innocently.

'Crivens, no!' shouted out Scott, taking a few deep breaths, 'it wisnae the answer that came to me, it was that woman again,' he coughed, as if trying to expunge the remnants of her air from his lungs.

'Oh, dear, I feared she might, that's why I've been staying so close to you. Maybe we should rescind the bathroom rule?'

'Maybe, or perhaps I'll just keep one eye open when showering in the future,' replied Scott, now calming down. 'Wait a minute, she spoke for longer this time, she spoke the words of the drum beat, it sounded like she knew their meaning; it sounded like she was repeating "rubidub dum, rubidub dum". At first I thought it sounded French, but when I tried to calm down and concentrate it sounded more Scottish, she was really rolling those rrr's, she had a right burr in her voice. Could she have been letting me know that the person beating the drum is from Britain, and not France?'

'Sorry you had to go through that Scott, but yes, he isn't a French drummer boy, he's one of ours, or rather one of yours.'

'One of mine? I dinnae ken fit you mean Naomi,' quickly replied Scott in his native Doric for I don't know what you mean. Upon hearing his own Scot's burr, a switched on lightbulb moment went off in his head. 'Of course! How could I have been sae stupid, fit a dunderheid I am. You mean a fellow Scot, whoa, wait a minute, aye, the Gordon Highlanders, my local Regiment in their time, served at Waterloo, they were known as the 92nd Regiment of Foot.' Scott looked around, hoping he was right and that the drummer boy would finally show himself and that then Scott could talk with him face to face, lay him to rest and no longer hear the beating drums in his head. He was bitterly disappointed as he heard "RUBIDUB DUM, RUBIDUB DUM," vibrate around the room. 'Ach!' he tutted.

'You still hear them, but cannot see him?' asked Naomi, though she already knew the answer.

'Aye,' replied Scott despondently his shoulders drooping, 'why couldn't it have been that easy?' he sighed. 'Will I ever get peace and quiet? But what's the connection between a wild looking woman in Tidworth and a drummer boy from Aberdeenshire?'

'Let me show you him, I'll take you to him. Hold my hand Scott.'

'Maybe let me get dressed first lass!'

Chapter 28

It was almost as if he could feel her soft skin wrapped delicately in his hands.

He closed his eyes and drew in their warmth, their suppleness, he moved his

fingers up and down hers wishing that it was their bodies thrusting and relaxing

together as if they were making love. But then his peace was shattered by the

explosive roar of the cannon as it pumped backwards, shaking the earth under

the gunners. Its deadly ball ejaculated and flew swiftly through the air,

decimating all in its path. Scott watched fascinated as the crew, eight of them to

this one cannon, sprang back into action.

The spongeman was already at the mouth of the cannon. He gave the huge

metal monster no time to draw breath or cool down. He thrust his wet, still

dripping shaft down into the depths of its barrel so as to quickly kill any dying

embers from the explosive fire. The sheepskin on the end of his cylinder shaped

pole quickly stemmed its ardour, extinguishing its lust for blood.

The loader, as practiced so many times, was immediately behind him and first

checked that the ventsman had his thumb over the vent at the rear end of the

barrel to prevent any air getting in and causing a premature explosion. No

sizzling embers would be responsible for taking his life today. Satisfied, he

quickly stuffed a new cartridge of gunpowder, a sealed bag of horror, down the

sizzling barrel, steam almost obscuring his vision as he tried to see beyond the white smoke that billowed in the air like a threatening cloud. He heaved a fresh twelve-pound ball of weight in after the flesh and bone damaging gunpowder, knowing that this would travel further in these opening minutes of the battle, to an enemy still too far away for musket fire. His crew had waited patiently until the battle attack order had been received from His Imperial Majesty. Napoleon had waited for the ground to dry after last night's rain. And now it was raining metal upon the skies above the British, Dutch and German infantry who were amassed only about 1700 yards away.

With a nod from the loader, the ventsman knew that the shot and cartridge had been successfully loaded. He pushed his pricker into the vent and pierced the deadly payload of the cartridge and ensured some of the gunpowder came with his retreating hand and was safely spread through the hole. With a swift and deft hand movement he then inserted the little firing tube, pre-filled with finely grained gunpowder. He quickly withdrew, crossing himself and thanking God that he still had his thumb and that this risky manoeuvre had not taken it as it had so many before. The cannon was now primed and ready for his detachment's commander.

He was responsible for adjusting the screw behind the barrel which elevated the gun. Once satisfied he shouted out "Feu" to his fellow Frenchmen. And fire they did, hundreds of times that day on the 18th June 1815, from their Grande Batterie, on a Belgium field so far away from both sides home countries.

The firer ran forward with his slow burning match and quickly lit the firing tube. The resulting explosion propelled the ball towards the Allied Armies lines, whilst the cannon was spat furiously six feet back into the dried muddy field. The three loading assistants sprang into action and with the help of their heavy work horses managed to drag the cannon back into place.

All this took just thirty seconds and Scott stared fascinated at this lethal destructive weapon. This early in the battle, thought by so many for so long, to have been an 11am start, would see the crew refreshed, for Emperor Napoleon always insisted his men sleep well the night before an intended battle, deliver two deadly loads a minute. Just from one gun. He had amassed 36 of these "belles filles" – his beautiful daughters, this morning and as his crews tired they would still fire a decimating 20 rounds each, per hour. In addition, the area, and many lives, would be devastated by 142 of his six-pounders and 68 howitzers that had a higher trajectory and could lob iron spheres packed with explosives and musket balls above the Allies heads. The resulting high velocity flying shards from the primed fuse hurtled down and ripped through flesh and fractured bones as easily as snapping a twig once it burned down and exploded. They were the most feared of weapons due to the high casualty rate.

On the Allies side, one artillery officer spotted Napoleon, distinct in his green coat with red facings. It was his gleaming white breeches and waistcoats that had attracted the artillery officer's attention. He knew it was definitely him when he saw the bicorne hat he favoured. The French leader was oblivious to his danger, he was too busy taking a measure of snuff and shaking the remains of the powder from his fingers. He turned to the Duke of Wellington, who wore leather nankeen pantaloons trousers, a white stock around his neck and wrapped up warm in his famous blue tailcoat and cocked hat, and said, 'permission to fire on His Imperial Majesty, the Emperor of France sir?' He had hoped to single handily have the prestige of finishing the battle and claiming Bonaparte's life.

'No! No! It is not the business of commanders to be firing upon each other!' was the response from his leader.

'You are quite safe Scott, these are just memories playing out, just like at the Battle of Loos when the Grey Lady took you there,' reassured Naomi. 'The battle of Waterloo has just begun; I shall take you to the Allied lines in just a moment.'

Scott marvelled at the stupidity of men, always fighting wars. In a hundred years the Germans, in this time called the Prussians, would no longer be allied with Britain, but would be their enemies. He had seen the destruction first hand at the Battle of Loos one hundred years and three months later; where the French would now be an Ally. His thoughts were interrupted by the sight of the ammunition wagons trundling towards the heavy cannons, laden with more deadly force which included flare shells for lighting up targets should the battle progress late into the summer evening and six or nine-pounder balls for nearer targets as the battle progressed. There would also be canister, or case shot as it was called by some, balls packed with sawdust in a tin or light case which fired deadly loads of packed musket balls up to four hundred yards. It would scatter its deadly payload out in a cone shaped formation scattering and causing great injuries like a shotgun blast, but on a larger scale. These would be saved for the later hours of the battle, as troops neared each other because its range was not as great. The heavycase or grapeshot as it was most commonly called contained less balls, but these were so much bigger; and deadlier. Scott wondered if Henry Shrapnel, the 1784 inventor of this wicked weapon, came to regret the conception. The wagons on the Allied side were also loaded with incendiary shells that could set fire to buildings and dry grassland and vegetation. Scott recalled reading that Napoleon had not thought to use these on the easily lit and combustible chateau and farmhouses of Hougoumont and La Haye Sainte until later in the day. Both would later play such pivotal roles in the Duke of Wellington's victory later this evening. Strange he thought, given that Napoleon Bonaparte trained as an artillery officer in his early military career.

'So you really can take me to any battle in history?'

'Yes Scott,' replied Naomi a little disappointed in his continuing lack of faith in her, 'and to any part of the battles. You have an advantage that any military commander would give their right arm for; you can see the action from both sides.'

Scott's eyes lit up, 'I've always wanted to see the defensive power of a square formation. I've read about them and seen them in films, but never in my wildest dreams would I have thought to see one live, well apart from in small re-enactments, but on this scale, wow!'

Naomi sighed; he really was living the dream now. All his earlier fears and frights had gone, as forgotten as a distant lover. 'Remember, we are here to show you the drummer boy, you need to understand his life, his death and most of all to get an understanding of his emotions.'

'Aye, aye, but gee whizz, just look at them all, look how magnificent these amassed armies are. There are thousands on each side. Do you know how many there are?'

'Historians have argued over this for years, but the most accurate figures are thought to be 54,400 infantry and 15,600 cavalry amassed by the French. The Allies mustered less, 53,800 troops and 13,350 cavalry. These don't include the support staff like the regimental cobblers and armourers. And remember, Napoleon's men were well trained, many of Wellington's men were not seasoned campaigners of the Napoleonic War; they were still fighting in America. That's why he mixed the Allies up, so that veterans would be fighting alongside those who had never fired a shot in battle before. You can't see all of them, though Scott, remember Wellington's love for ridges? He has many more beyond that rise and many more will soon be galloping and marching to his call. Hold my hand again Scott; let me take you to him.'

'Keep it together,' yelled the sergeant a forlorn hope survivor. With twenty-four other men he had been the first through a breach in a defensive bastion wall three years ago at Badajoz in Spain. He had been the only survivor and had more than earned his stripes. His subaltern, the Lieutenant, had been the first shot and killed by the enemy that day and with his life gone so was the chance of commanding his own company. The sergeant would never again volunteer for such a storming party, no matter how well the engineers had broken the defences. He didn't want to be one of those gibbering wrecks left to soil themselves all day and night in the military asylum. Sadly, some from this battle would end up at the Fort Clarence Military Asylum in Rochester and then see out their days at the military asylum at Hoxton. Nor would he allow this misfit bunch of men to cost him his life. 'Bunch up, I will flay alive the first man that moves!'

Scott admired the way the sergeant commanded his men, through sheer fear, but for their own good. They looked resplendent in their red jackets and white cross belts, their black stocks worn tightly at their necks. They were amassed four ranks deep, two companies to each side in a classic defensive position against the French cavalry; their lethal cuirassiers. They were much feared by the British because they had never faced them in Spain, during the Peninsular War. They had only heard horror stories and hoped that they would not come at them with their huge chargers, the thick set and powerful horses that were exclusively bred in Normandy. Each soldier looked resplendent in their blue uniforms, and with black horse-hair plumes proudly displayed from their helmets, and the tell-tale give-away of the sun glinting on their shiny yellow steel breastplates which were rumoured to be bulletproof. Though in reality they may stop the round fired from a pistol, they offered little protection against rifle and musket fired at a higher velocity.

The front two ranks would kneel as the French charged on their giant horses, the earth pounding and thundering beneath the horses' hooves, the vibrations heard by their enemy; putting the fear of God into each of them. Each cavalryman of this elite French unit, rumoured to be over six feet tall, would wield their long straight edged swords, designed to keep the British curved sabres at bay, hoping to thrust and impale and disembowel their enemies. The Allies in turn would hope their defensive square would cause the horses to hesitate and stumble at the sight of the two ranks that would brace the ends of their muskets into the ground allowing their razor sharp bayonets to point upwards. Horses would refuse to be led there, and the few that did would be shot by the rear ranks that were ready to fire, having already primed and loaded their Baker rifles. Any cuirassier who was thrown by their horse would be easy pickings for the Allies; their heavy plating and jackboots would hold them to the ground causing them to sprawl and kick like overturned tortoises, until finished off by the knives and bayonets of soldiers wishing to preserve their ammunition from this easy prey. This was the main reason why British cavalry units did not wear armour; they relied instead on superior speed, manoeuvrability and agility.

Sadly, though, for these brave foot soldiers, the square would be no defence against the artillery that continued to bombard them. The cuirassiers, who from a distance looked like jousting medieval knights, would not challenge the square until this afternoon, long after many in the square had lost their lives, or had been taken back to the surgeons for limb amputations.

Scott watched in morbid fascination as they formed square. They were soon bombarded, helpless to do anything but watch for the incoming deadly loads. He let out an inappropriate laugh.

Naomi looked at him puzzled, 'what on earth are you finding to laugh about?'

'Watch them closely lass.'

She looked more carefully and could soon see what he had found amusing.

'Sorry lass, I know good men lost their lives but look at them bobbing and weaving, ducking and diving. That row just bent down in one line, one after the other like a Mexican wave.'

'They are seeing optical illusions Scott,' explained Naomi patiently, 'the twelve-pounder balls fired at them appear as large black dots, even when they are far off. They think it's about to hit their faces, but what they are actually seeing is it bouncing towards them with such speed. Watch.'

The laugh and grin soon disappeared from Scott as the first of many cannonballs hit the front rank who had no time to kneel. Its momentum took a head clean off as the skull bounced into the head of the man behind him and fractured his jaw. Others were splattered with grey and red matter which warmed their face and obscured their vision. The salt of the blood was tasted by those whose mouths were open. In the next line a soldier was eviscerated as the force of the shot went straight through his abdomen, opened up his rib cage and splattered his entrails onto the earth in a steaming pile, like a dropped link of sausages in a butcher's shop. He plummeted to the floor like a downed skittle in a macabre game of bowls. Two soldiers behind him, in the third rank, suffered fractured femurs as the same cannonball ploughed on; they tried desperately to stay upright by grasping at the men to their sides and yelled screaming in excruciating pain as their nerve endings sent rapid messages to their befuddled brains. The square had fallen and the cannon ball was still not spent.

A guardsman in the rear rank, known to be the joker of the regiment, saw the ball start to lose its momentum and shouted out, 'here, lads, I know how to stop it!' His colleague to his right realised what he intended and was too late to stop him. The joker stuck out his foot, as if trapping a football that had been passed on a pitch. His shoe, complete with foot, flew into the air. Blood pumped out between the two shattered bones of his lower leg and he dropped to the floor and bled out before he could reach the safety of the surgeons and their petit screw tourniquet and surgery without anaesthetic or analgesia. Perhaps this way was luckier for him?

'Bunch up, stand firm and stand fast,' barked the sergeant, oblivious to the slaughter.

'That's the most devastating carnage I've ever seen,' said Scott, mouth agape and looking ashen.

'It doesn't get any better. Let me take you to another square.'

The drummer boy stood in the middle of the square, a hollowed area that offered the best protection for important men and officers. He was afforded this limited sanctuary because soon, very soon, he would have to beat his drums and direct the men to advance upon the enemy. He awaited his commands of prepare to fire, form square, march, assembly, advance or retreat from the colonel. But his fingers were not still, they shook with fear and vibrated against the skin of his drum, though the sound was not heard above the whistling echoes of multiple cannon fire and bursts of explosions. He cried out the only word that someone in his position would as he felt the wetness soil his kilt again, 'mummy.'

He hoped that the enemy skirmishers, the French elite voltigeurs with their yellow plumes and blue uniforms that looked like darting budgerigars, would not be skirting around them, ready to fire an opportune shot at the officers, sergeants, corporals or him. These best shooters of the enemy were trained to shoot at the leaders, drummers and trumpeters first, so that troops could not be rallied or commanded. Their objective was to spread fear and disorganisation.

He looked nervously about him for the tell-tale darting yellow plumes of these small agile men. He prayed they would not spot him through the sights of their rifled carbines. He hoped that Napoleon had not yet released his Tiraileurs of the Imperial Guard who had an even deadlier reputation for sharp shooting.

He cast nervous eyes around him hoping not to see the half ounce ball that could so easily end his young life and he selfishly hoped that they were busy trying to do what they always did first, despite their orders. That was to kill the Allied skirmishers first during a cunning cat and mouse game of self-preservation.

After the death of her husband, she did not wish to marry another soldier of the regiment straight away, as was the custom. She was no longer able to be a camp follower, the group of lucky wives, with their children, selected at random, to follow behind and earn their keep by cooking, doing the laundry and mending uniforms. Instead she offered her son up as a drummer boy, she little suspected the danger he would be in. She had naively thought he would beat a tune for them to march, be fed and cared for, whilst she was bound for the workhouse. She can't have known that he would be right in the thick of the battle, could she...

'There, look, between the officer on the horse and the standard bearer, there he is,' shouted out Naomi above the sounds of battle, the screaming of wounded men, the barking of orders and the incessant cannon fire.

'I see him, he's got a tall black hairy bearskin hat on, the poor wee soul looks terrified, all wide eyed and lost. Christ, but he only looks about eight, maybe ten. I always thought drummer boys were veterans, too old to fight, but kept on by regiments as a reward for good service.'

'No Scott, that's a common misconception. They were not mascots. They had to be alert, of good hearing, swift and agile. Their young ears weren't too damaged by the noise of gunfire like most veterans. Most were orphans. They were put in vulnerable positions because they had to be near to the commanders, ready to relay orders through their drums. Enemy soldiers were trained to fire at them, to take out the leader, drummers and trumpeters. Men without leaders would then become directionless and confused. It was quite a risky role. Many were wounded and killed. The French would target them. There would be six per battalion due to their high fatality rate. Other drummer boys would be used as ammunition carriers and to pass water to the troops, biting the gritty gunpowder cartridges would make them thirsty. That's why their mouths and faces are all black. Some even dislocated their shoulders from the constant firing and recoil of their muskets. At the very least the survivors would have heavily bruised shoulders by the end of the fighting. The drummer boys would also need to carry water to the men so that they could clean through their rifle chambers that got clogged quickly by the gunpowder, although many did this by urinating down the barrels. I wonder if our drummer boy survived this battle or got wounded and eventually shipped home. I wonder what took him to Tidworth, perhaps we'll never know. I hope we find out.'

'The poor wee laddie, and that's who's been haunting me all these months. He looks so harmless, so afraid. But why won't he show himself to me, why does he just beat his drums in my head?'

'Because you are not ready to believe Scott, I know you said not to mention it, but you need your faith.'

'Seeing all this carnage, this needless death, how can God allow this?'

'God doesn't. He gives men and women free will and full rein for their actions. It is mankind who chooses to go to war. That is why soldiers go to heaven Scott. The 453 remember? We fought what we hoped was a just war in Afghanistan. We believed we were fighting to stop the rise of the Taliban and to stop the poppy seed reaching our kids in Britain. We thought, wrongly as it turns out, that Blair led us justly through Iraq because there were weapons of mass destruction. Saddam needed stopping. We were just in our actions. Not murderers. They go to hell because they have evil in their hearts; not good. It's all about faith Scott, everything is, especially your future.'

'I try too, but my feelings, my anger stops me.'

'I know my love, but let your love for me shine through you and restore your faith.'

Changing the subject quickly Scott asked, 'take me to the chateau farm, take me to Hougoumont. I want to show you human compassion in the heat of battle, take me to the place where Wellington said "the success of the battle of Waterloo depended on the closing of the gates of Hougoumont." I want to see if he really was as big as they say he was.'

'Who?' asked a puzzled Naomi.

'Ah, not all-seeing and knowing then, let me surprise you this time. Take my hand now,' commanded Scott.

Naomi took them about 300 yards from the front line where the noise was still deafening, only it was a different sort of noise. It was the sound of Baker rifles and muskets being primed and loaded. An assortment of pings and bangs from the Land, India and New Land Pattern muskets added to the cacophony of noise that resembled the smoke and noise from an enthusiastic fireworks display. Those lucky enough to be issued or those who "acquired" their Baker rifles benefited from being able to fire a shorter-barrelled weapon. Its seven turns within the barrel ensured that the bullet spun through the chamber and gave it a longer range. It was also more accurate and could pierce a man's heart at two-hundred yards. It was usually only issued to those in the British army who were able to fire upon enemy officers and drummers, such as the 95th Rifles. It still had to be fired by a flintlock musket, like the smooth bore muskets with 39 inch barrels which were nicknamed the Brown Bess. These were for close quarter fighting.

'Watch how quickly they load their weapons,' said Scott in admiration.

Naomi watched as a rifleman inside the defended farmhouse building flicked open his priming pan and took out a paper cartridge. He bit it open and put a small amount of the gunpowder into the casing and flicked it shut. He quickly upended his rifle and poured the remaining gunpowder down its barrel. Then he spat a greasy powder encrusted bullet, which was ball shaped, that he had held in his teeth down the barrel. In a smooth action he withdrew the ramrod from below the barrel and placed it in the muzzle of the musket and rammed home the ball and gunpowder. He then pulled back the cock of the rifle which was behind the flint, aimed and pulled the trigger. One of the attacking Frenchmen dropped down dead.

'Blimey, I could have fired a whole magazine on automatic in that time,' said an unimpressed Naomi. 'Where's the compassion you talked about?'

'Patience, lass, this is the battle during a battle. Waterloo was more than just that day; it was spread over four days at places like Quatre Bras. Wellington was a great strategist, despite Napoleon "humbugging him" by crossing the Belgium border and into Charleroi whilst he was at the Duchess of Richmond's Ball on the 15th June. Mind you, with many of his officers there he used it to his advantage and turned the social occasion into an orders group and got one of his aides to distribute movement orders. Pipe Major Alexander Cameron and four Gordon Highlander sergeants gave an outstanding sword dance apparently, just before the Duke arrived at 11pm.'

Naomi looked even more confused; clearly she needed to brush up a bit on Waterloo history.

'That loading and firing was considered really fast for its day. A well-practiced rifleman could fire off three or four rounds a minute, look.'

Naomi watched as one rifleman poured down his gunpowder and spat out the ball and instead of ramming it home he thumped the back of the musket down twice in quick succession onto the ground, drew back the cocking mechanism and fired. Another Frenchmen lay dying.

'Of course Wellington frowned on such risky practices, in case the flint ignited the powder. But experienced riflemen new lots of tricks like that. Most would throw away and replace their flints after firing 30 rounds, usually by taking it from a dead comrade's gun. That's where the term to go off half-cocked comes from by the way. During some skirmishes or marches into enemy-held territory the troops would pre-prime and load their rifles and muskets. That way they were ready to quickly return fire if ambushed. The trick was to cock the rifle and then cover the cocking mechanism with some cloth so that the rifle wouldn't go off accidentally and shoot one of their own in front. The cloth also kept the powder dry.'

Naomi pointed to the ground, 'why are there so many playing cards scattered about?'

'It was considered bad luck to have them. Soldiers thought the cards would attract musket balls. So they always threw away any packs of cards before a battle. They thought they had to throw them over their heads and not look back to be free of the bad luck. Some even went as far as swallowing gunpowder or one of the round bullets, thinking that if they already had a bullet or gunshot in them, then they wouldn't get shot. You know how superstitious soldiers can be. The other bits and pieces scattered around is unwanted heavy baggage from their packs, so that they can move quicker. If they survived, they'd simply loot what they need from the dead, along with any coins and jewellery, even teeth. They would later sell them in London. They were known as the Waterloo Teeth, the rich who loved the expensive sugar would use them as dentures. Some full sets fetched up to twenty guineas. Some were even set in hippopotamus ivory as a base.'

'You've still got it, haven't you?'

'Mm,' replied a distracted Scott, wanting to watch the quick-loader in action a bit more.'

'What your mother gave you, as a small boy.'

Scott withdrew a well-thumbed black object from his pocket, his lucky black cat trinket, given to his mother when she was first in hospital. She told him that if he always carried it with him, then no harm could happen to him. She still died though, he thought bitterly. 'Aye, it comes everywhere with me, daft really,' he shrugged.

Naomi knew he was thinking of his mother, and also that he wasn't daft. It had kept him from so much harm. 'So why is this area so important?'

It was the western flank of the battlefield, a large bastion of buildings used as a defensive shield against French attack on Wellington's right side. He ordered that it be defended to the utmost; he even had the foresight to place a supply of spare ammunition in the buildings, something not usually done. It was the Coldstream Guards that worked together with the German Legion pioneers, late the night before and early in the morning. They knocked through loopholes in

212

the walls to use as firing positions and built shooting platforms above. You'll see why in a minute. There were only two-hundred guardsmen defending this vital position, though they were later joined on that ridge over there by two light companies. When one of his aides-de-camp questioned if two-hundred guardsmen were enough in the buildings Wellington replied "Ah, but you don't know Macdonell." He was their lieutenant-colonel; the men would have followed him anywhere. Wellington referred to him as the bravest man in the army. He proved it that day too at that 16th Century Chateau du Goumont.

Before the battle there was a well-stocked dovecote upon a disused and capped well. The pigeons and doves took to the roofs when the firing started. They flew off and after the battle came straight back as if nothing had happened; they sat cooing and watching, miraculously untouched.'

'Blimey, but your dad's birds fly off at the least noise.'

'Aye and these poor things were then shot and roasted for supper after the battle. Ramrods were used as useful roasting tools. Dead cuirassiers breastplates, scavenged from the battlefield, made helpful roasting trays. It was the first proper meal some had eaten in days, other than the stir-about porridge to which anything foraged would be added. So maybe dad's pigeons are wiser. There was also a walled garden that the French needed to break through. But this was defended by more Allied troops, the Hanoverian riflemen, the elite Jagers. They earned their reputation that day. The battle within the battle started at about 11:30am, soon after the initial bombardment of the main battlefield, and the Colonel and all the troops held out against the French infantry columns and their skirmishers. It was Napoleon's brother, Jerome, who led the attack. He led fourteen-thousand men and still the Allies held on, but it was close. Even when the buildings burnt down after the French finally used incendiary devices from their howitzers the Allies retreated to the Chapel which was still standing and defended it. Some say Waterloo could have been won by Napoleon if his brother had only used some of his men to reinforce Marshal Ney. The attack on the chateau was only supposed to be a French diversion. By the afternoon fourteen-thousand French troops were killed, wounded or pinned down by the surrounding Allied troops that numbered no more than three-thousand-five-hundred. That was about a fifth of Napoleon's army against the might of thirty-four year old Colonel Macdonnell; no wonder Wellington had such great faith in him.'

'You've had too much time on your hands to read about Waterloo, you should get out more. Where's this big man you were talking about?'

'Aye well, that was during Colonel Cubieres assault on the north gate. Let's go there.'

'Who died and made you the boss?' quibbled Naomi.

'Do you see him now,' enthused Scott.

'Fuck me! He's bloody huge'

Scott frowned, 'for an angel you've got a right potty mouth.'

Naomi shrugged, 'I never said I was perfect! If that's how tall he is, imagine how big his c…'

'Never mind that, interrupted Scott, be quiet and watch. His name is Legros, though some say Le Gros. His real name was Bonnet. He's a Sous-Lieutenant and he was nicknamed l'enfonceur which translates to the smasher.'

'I'm not surprised; look at the size of that bloody axe he's carrying.' The penny dropped, 'his job is to smash through the gates. Then Napoleon can march his troops and wheel his cannon through.'

'Aye,' said Scott, 'the roads were few around here and there was no way that the heavy cannon and horses could get through the muddy fields. Wellington knew what he was about. Normally pioneer axes like that would be used to chop down trees.'

'Legros was a former sergeant in the engineers. And like many troops when Napoleon marched back through France to Paris to dethrone King Louis XVIII after his escape from exile in Elba, he quickly re-joined the French army and was promoted.'

'He's running through that rifle fire without a care in the world, not one bullet has found its mark. He's untouched. But their Colonel Cubieres horse has been shot, it's trapped him, it's a dead weight. Why don't the Allies finish him off? The French will then be leaderless.'

'He thought that the British commanding officer was gentlemanly and commanded his troops not to fire on a vulnerable officer. Who knows, perhaps he was chivalrous. Do you see how some of the French have got through, perhaps a dozen?'

'Yes, but Colonel Macdonnell is running across with his men, with heavy logs, they are trying to bar the gate. But some of the French are still inside. So is the big man with the axe. Fuck Me!' swore Naomi again as a head went bouncing past her, trailing a stream of blood from the collapsing torso.

Legros swung the pioneer axe again, carving through a rifleman's shoulder with the ease of a butcher preparing a joint for a Sunday roast dinner, though this scene was far from homely. He raised his huge right foot, placed it on the dying man's groin and pushed and forced his bloodied axe out from his bones and flesh.

One lucky Frenchman fired off a round which went clean through a Captain's arm before a volley of rounds tore into his torso from the defensive position above.

Whilst Legros was in mid swing to carve through another rifleman the giant of a Frenchman was shot dead as all around him there was hand-to-hand fighting. A British sergeant, knowing he didn't have time to reload, turned over his rifle with haste and used the stock to club to death the nearest Frenchman, only stopping when white mush oozed out from the man's caved in head.

'There,' shouted Scott, 'there is humanity and compassion, look to the French drummer boy who was swept along with his comrades.'

She looked on as a young lad, no more than 12 years of age, stood screaming at the wanton carnage around him. His drumsticks fell from his hands as he clasped his ears, as if to drown out the screams of the dying. An English private ran to him, dodging French thrusts of swords, bayonets and rifle butts. He scooped up the drummer boy in one fell swoop and sprinted him off to the safety of the nearest building. The battle continued during this heroic rescue as British junior officers withdrew their swords from their scabbards to the sound of metal upon metal and sliced their way through their enemy. In a frenzy of battle-lust the last of the Frenchmen fell at the hands of the Coldstream Guards and Hanoverians. German soldiers fighting alongside British troops as Brothers in Arms. That would change within the Century thought Scott wryly again. The Colonel, along with brothers and Corporals James and Joseph Graham, heaved, but the gates would not budge until they were joined by four men of the 3rd Foot Guard who squeezed through the melee and aided them. With a final push the men slowly forced the gates closed against the mass of the French who had finally reached them. The locking-bar was eventually put in place. The gates were securely shut and they had successfully barricaded themselves against the attackers: Hougoumont had narrowly escaped being taken and about 100 French corpses littered the courtyard. Their only survivor was the terrified drummer boy. He would no longer play the pas de charge.

This didn't stop the French outside and some climbed on comrade's shoulders in an effort to shoot down into the courtyard. They made trouble for the

Riflemen until General Byng on the ridge saw that reinforcements were needed and sent the 2nd Battalion Coldstream Guards down the hill to counter-attack and drive off the French. This was just the beginning of the battle, the longest day in the lives of survivors.

'I don't want to see any more fighting Scott, all that bloodshed is too much, even for me. Let's go back, I think I've shown you enough of the drummer boy's life for you to understand his fear, what he lived through.'

'Aye lass, but let's have a wee look at the medical care first, I want to see if it's as brutal as the fighting.'

'After the battle a lot of the surgeons wanted to come across to Belgium from Britain. They wanted the experience of caring for wounds that they'd not see in their cosy hospitals and even worked here without pay in the six hospitals that were set up within the week at Brussels,' explained Scott. Just in this area alone two thousand five hundred wounded soldiers were treated. The same number of soldiers was cared for at Antwerp. More hospitals opened up in Bruges, Ostend and Gwent. The St Joseph Church in the village of Waterloo was used on the day of the battle and for days afterwards as a hospital. People like Charles Bell, who named the Bell's nerve and palsy, vastly increased their knowledge. He went as far as making sure that the French were treated as equally well as the Allies. He took lots of notes that changed the way surgeons thought and worked. He was quite the pioneer. His water-colour paintings are preserved at the Royal College of Surgeons in Edinburgh and at the University College London buildings. Seventeen of them, along with his notebook, were presented to the Royal Hospital in Netley, the old army hospital where the park and chapel now sit, by his widow.'

'I've seen some Scott, the chest wound one was fascinating, such detail. But don't you want to see the real work, the place where the butcher's list, the number of the dead and wounded, are counted?'

'Aye, but I thought you'd be more interested in going back to one of the Square's first, to see one of the surgeon's performing first aid.'

'I've seen that before Scott, I had a lot of time on my hands when you were in your coma. They had their trusted box chest containing a harrowing assortment of saws, knives, blades, bullet forceps, bone nippers and even cupping sets and leeches. It was barbaric field medicine, mostly to try and retrieve the round bullets or to amputate decimated limbs before gangrene set in. Remarkably none of the surgeons in the squares were killed, such was the defence abilities of these formations. They carried out quick surgery as all hell was let loose around them. Even padres found themselves in squares, like the fighting padre, Edward Frith. He earned his nickname because he would preach to the men mid-battle. He really stirred the men up. Every regiment was supposed to have one padre from the Army Chaplains Department. They were established in 1796 and were initially recruited from the Church of England. Wellington would not allow Methodists, he thought they were subversive. Only six padres made it to Belgium.'

'Aye, those were the bravest surgeons and padres, but even those in the temporarily field hospitals were so near the frontline. There was no recognised chain of evacuation as such, it was only four days earlier that the War Office had reappointed Sir James McGrigor as head of the medical service to prepare the medical services for an invasion of France. Men tried to leave the battlefield on the excuse of taking wounded men to surgeons, and some took the opportunity to flee. Captain Mercer of the Horse Artillery would later claim that he saw ten or more Belgians attending to just one wounded soldier. British soldiers joked that the colourful Belgian orange and white hats with the W badge for King William of the Netherlands were peaked on both the front and back so that you couldn't tell if they were coming or going. There was a major rout to Brussels. There was even a team of junior surgeons and musicians who were acting as medical orderlies who joined them in deserting their hospital post near the windmill at Mont Saint-Jean.'

'Cowards,' cursed Naomi, 'surely they weren't British?'

'No, these were from the Hanoverian militia; they were simply overwhelmed at the devastation they witnessed. That's why the rumours spread.'

'Rumours?' questioned Naomi.

'Aye, as they made their way to Brussels on foot, or cart if they were lucky, they talked to passers-by and told them that Napoleon was winning. That's why many thought Wellington had lost, though the battle was still being fought. If it wasn't for the Prussians mind you, he may well have lost. Wellington called it "the nearest run thing you ever saw in your life." Marshall Prince Blucher and his troops came at the eleventh hour and saved Wellington's bacon. Together they were able to make a final attack using artillery, cavalry and infantry, but at a cost. There was a 30% casualty rate. During the Peninsular War this was only about 10% for most battles. The numbers have been discussed for decades, but I think there were about 3500 dead, 3300 missing and 10,200 wounded, just from

Wellington's troops. And many wounded would die days later and some of those numbered as missing were found later to be dead, after the confusion of battle. There were so many buried at Waterloo that it was said by many years later that the ground was still springy underfoot. Some officers, like Colonel John Cameron, were taken home, their bodies preserved in barrels of rum. He was the 92nd Gordon Highlander's Commanding Officer.'

'I've never been able to understand why the casualty rate was so high, surely they could have got the wounded out after the French fled?'

'Most of the troops were too fatigued to do anything other than eat or sleep. Others, like the artillerymen, were truly deaf to their plaintive cries in the night. There were no ear defenders for these gunners who fired all day long. It took artillerymen about three days to hear and some still even thought they could hear the roaring of the cannons days afterwards. No-one was assigned to pick out the wounded; they were left to die amongst the dead. It was pitch-dark by then, even though it was early summer. Many were helped on their way by looters, military and civilian folk who went by lantern light to rob; they even stripped the wounded of their clothes because most soldiers hid their coins and jewellery in the lice-ridden linings. Toothbrushes were a favourite find amongst the soldiers. Especially from the corpses of officers who could afford the horn handled ones set with hog bristle. A more thorough search of a body with one of these could result in finding the matching lice comb. Otherwise it was back to using a twig with split ends to clean gums and teeth. The provosts, showing no quarter, did shoot some of them as a warning to others, but by the morning many of the dead had been stripped bare. Some of the luckier wounded did get taken off the battlefield, their cries alerting conscientious comrades, but they were few and far between. Some locals even sold swords to the tourists that came within days of the battle. Famous folk like Lord Byron, Sir Walter Scott and Robert Peel came to look around, often given a guided tour by locals. They fair made money.'

'That's awful Scott.'

'Aye, different times I guess. One guide, called Decoster, claimed that Napoleon forced him to be an informer during the battle. He said he had to tell him about the lay of the land. He made a lot of money from the tourists in the years after the battle. Many of the tourists came to see the faces, arms and legs that stuck out of the communal burial plots. They hadn't buried the soldiers deep enough you see. That was before that big Lion Mound was erected to show where Prince William of Orange was wounded. His father had the landscape carved up so that the battlefield no longer looks like it did on the day. That wasn't the first time the dead were disturbed in their graves though because many locals dug up the area looking for souvenirs to sell. But there was some great work done by surgeons, often working around the clock, it took them days to tend to the wounded, the lucky ones who made it back to care. They earned their Chelsea Commission. Back at the Elizabeth Hospital in Brussels the first amputated hip joint operation was performed by British military surgeon

George Guthrie. He operated on a Frenchman prisoner of war called Francois. He survived and was even cared for by the same surgeon when he was taken to York Hospital in Chelsea five months later. Although some at Mont Saint-Jean fled, there were also British surgeons working in a farmyard nearby, like Haddy James of the 1st Life Guards. He worked all day and night to save lives. He later wrote such a moving tribute to the soldiers under his care:

"It was grim in the extreme and continued far into the night. It was all too horrible to commit to paper, but this I will say, that the silent heroism of the greater part of the sufferer was a thing I shall not forget. When one considers the hasty surgery performed on such an occasion, the awful sight the men are witness to, knowing that their turn on that blood soaked operating table is next, seeing the agony of an amputation, however swiftly performed, and the longer torture of a probing, then one realised fully what our soldiers are made."

Naomi wiped a tear from her eye and reached out for Scott's hand, 'come, we should see this for ourselves.'

Straw and animal muck lay on the cobbled floor, splattered with the blood and entrails of dying and dead men. Through the gate a bandsman, his ornate uniform grimy with mud and dried blood had his arm around a man, practically dragging him into the courtyard. The man's right arm was drooping down across his abdomen, not because it had been shot, but because he was trying desperately to keep his bowels together. His stomach had been sliced open and he was hopelessly juggling layers of bowel, trying to cram it back into his open wound, like rearranging slippery eels in a bucket. His face was contorted in pain and he was crying out desperately for his wife. He would die within the hour; his liver had been punctured. He was placed, gently, onto the floor amongst other men, whose uniform were in tatters, some with parts of their hands, arms, feet and legs missing, stumps wrapped in an assortment of linen ransacked from the nearby farmhouse because the medical wagon, full of bandages, was still behind the lines.

Two surgeons were working back to back across hastily improvised operating tables, two thick oak doors taken from the adjacent building. The thick grain of the wood did nothing to stop the flow of the blood as patient after patient was heaved onto the makeshift bench and held down by four of the broadest bandsmen with the strongest stomachs. One was already heaving over his shoulder at the sight of the surgeon probing deep into a shoulder wound with first his bare finger and then his bullet forceps that no longer glinted in the dying day's sun for it was caked in crusted blood. He shook his head, threw down the instrument and casually scooped away fresh blood from his apron. He reluctantly picked up his saw with its last blade, now sadly blunted. He hoped that the man had at least drunk the customary pint of rum. Even the opium, stuck miles away in their medical wagon, wouldn't have stopped the pain anyway. Chloroform, an early anaesthetic, would not be accidentally discovered for at least another fifteen years and not used as a battlefield anaesthetic until the Battle of Alma during the Crimean War. The four bandsmen tightened their grip whilst the soldier begged the surgeon to spare his arm, offered him all the looted coins and trinkets from previous campaigns, he pleaded to deaf ears. The surgeon knew that in order to save this poor soul's life from blood poisoning his limb would have to come off. The surgeon took a deep breath and despite his aching arms, he had lost count of the number of limbs he had tossed into the pile soaking and rotting in the corner, he made it quick. Within seconds he was turning the petit screw tourniquet tighter. Sixty seconds later, after much biting on a piece of wood, the soldier had passed out; nature had been kind to him and given him reprieve and a natural anaesthetic, and the surgeon had finished his grisly task. He straightened up, nodded to the bandsmen and turned to the group of men and pointed to the next man he knew he could treat. Other bandsmen were bringing him whilst their comrades were taking the armless man through an archway to a room filled with straw flooring and the groans and moans of men who had helped blunt the saws of the two surgeons.

'Fuck! There's no other word for it Scott, this is grisly, and soldiers down the centuries have had to undergo this. Medical science may be very developed now and few will die like some here will from infection, but fuck me!'

'I ken lass; war is such horror. And these are the lucky ones. Most will make it back to the four hospitals that Wellington had set up at Brussels, but journeying there on basic carts is going to be rough and painful. The poor fellows, they have earned their medal.'

Scott had recently seen several of the Waterloo medals during a browse around the Army Medical Services Museum displays at Keogh Barracks in Ash Vale. These had been awarded to Assistant Surgeon Nicholaus D Meyer, who served with the 1st Dragoon and later the Light Dragoons of the King's German Legion, Assistant Surgeon Frederick B White, who served as Hospital Mate to the 2nd Battalion, 73rd Foot Regiment and had been promoted to Assistant Surgeon on 23rd March 1815 and Deputy Purveyor George Robinson, who served with the Department of Field Equipment. In the glass cabinet Scott had marvelled at the colours of the fading maroon which was sandwiched by blue ribbon on either side. One side of the round metal depicted the winged victory emblem and the other the head of the Prince Regent. He thought then and more so now that they were thoroughly well deserved by these and other brave men. Each was engraved with the name of the recipient around the rim and they were also given to widows and families of the dead. It was the very first medal to be awarded to the British Army by the Government, regardless of rank. Every soldier would receive two years seniority towards their pay and pension for their actions that day, known as the Prince Regent's bounty. Men could retire two years earlier on full pension. Two years after Waterloo they could also claim their share of the battle prize money, £2 for privates and £1275 for a general. The Duke of Wellington would always give a sovereign to any veteran he saw wearing the Waterloo medal. It would be another thirty-two years before the Peninsula medal was awarded, and most recipients were long dead.

But none of this mattered to the men who were dying, or wished they were dead, as their blood poured and over-spilled from the thick horizontal doors and ran onto the dirty floor like torrents of water gushing from a burst river and carving its own path through all that stood in its way.

'You don't see them, do you Scott?'

'Them, you mean the wounded soldiers, the surgeons and the orderlies, aye, I see them.'

'No. I didn't think you did. You didn't see them at the squares or the farmhouses either; otherwise you'd have said something.'

'I don't know what you mean lass.'

Naomi reached across to him, 'here, let me use just a small amount of my spiritual energy,' her hand glowing orange again. This time fine specks of ember glowing dust-like particles stretched across the space between them, rising up like a feather caught in the wind, and entered gently into his eyes. Scott blinked several times. 'That should help you see clearly now my darling.'

At the next blink Scott's sight became more focused and he took in the wondrous spectacular that Naomi now shared with him. Above and to either side of several of the soldiers were auburn glowing people, smiling and reaching out to the hands of those who were so obviously dying, as if to comfort them. 'Good Lord!' exclaimed Scott, 'What are they?'

'They are like me Scott, they are war angels assigned as guiding angels to bring comfort as the soldiers die, to shepherd them to heaven. They are their dead relatives, familiar faces who will ease them from this life to the next. They gain temporary entrance to this physical plain, just for a few minutes, near to the time of death. Many of these soldiers won't make it to the surgeon's table I'm afraid.'

'They are so beautiful; I've never seen such beauty in all my life, what an incredible sight. And you say these were also at the battle?'

'Yes Scott, at this battle, and every war throughout history. They also temporarily walk the streets, hospitals, hospices, woods, anywhere where there is death, civilian and military. God blessed them with this temporary power to ease safe passage to heaven for those who deserved ascension.'

'W.. would my mum have had one?' asked Scott in a low whisper, as if he did not want to disturb the ethereal wonder playing out before him.

'Yes my darling, she had many, her parents, your wonderful grandparents and other relatives and friends who have passed over. They filled her with such love and reassurance. That's why she died so peacefully, holding your and your dear father's hands. Do you remember the smile on her face as she drew her last breath?'

'Aye, she was at such peace. And I've seen such serenity in some of the patients I've nursed as they reached the end of their life, but bless me, I did not know of such wonders.'

'Few of the living are blessed with seeing them. But sometimes a dying person whispers names of those long gone and this is heard by the living. Now you know why. I hope this gives you some faith now Scott, I pray it truly does.'

'Aye, well, maybe, but I do miss mum, and my grandparents, they were such lovely folk.'

'And you will see them again one day Scott, but not just yet, your time is a long way off. Shall we go now; I think I'd like to end these scenes on this lovely image?'

'Aye,' replied Scott, not wanting to take his eyes away as he saw a young man, probably in his twenties, kneel down by someone who was most likely his father, whose arm had been shattered by musket balls. He was reaching out and stroking his father's hair, as if soothing a child after a terrible nightmare. A wave of pain passed over the soldier's face as if gently washed by a gentle tide lapping on a golden beach.

Scott sighed peacefully as if exhaling all bad memories, 'I don't want to leave, but I know I must, this abattoir has turned into a haven of tranquillity. God bless them all. Thank you for showing this to me Naomi. He suddenly looked shocked. 'But you're still here, despite transferring your powers to me. How has that happened?'

'Like you, I am growing stronger; we are bursting through our transitional period and leaping into exciting new chapters.'

'Just like Jake said!' exclaimed Scott. 'He was a funny ghost. I bet he's still making himself laugh, at the theatre staffs expense!'

'Yes, he's got a typical ex-soldier's humour. Civilians just don't get our sense of humour sometimes,' replied Naomi.

'Aye, just like all the soldiers here at Waterloo, there was still humour, despite all this carnage,' said Scott.

'Oh,' replied Naomi, still taking in the splendour of what was playing out in front of them, her angelic brethren, her new brothers and sisters.

'Aye. Let me tell you a quick story. Wellington's brother's wife ran off with Lord Uxbridge, who during this battle was the Commander of the Allied cavalry. So there was ill feeling between the two men. Anyway later in the battle some French case shot took off Uxbridge's right knee, just as the French were retreating. In shock he simply said, "By God sir! I've lost my leg." To which our Duke is said to have replied, "By God sir! So you have!" without pausing for breath.'

Chapter 31

'I can show you something even funnier Scott.'

'Oh aye, show me then lass,' replied Scott, glad too of being finally taken away from all the needless slaughter and butchery, though also reluctant to leave the splendour of the war angels. He took her ghostly hand once more, 'Where are we off to now lass?'

'Back to Tidworth, but forward in time, to 1976 at the Military Hospital, a year before it closed, you'll love this!'

'Have you wound them up enough then Malcolm?' asked Trevor, the other Corporal receptionist on duty this evening at the reception desk at the Tidworth Military Hospital. He was dressed in a thick green woollen jumper with two white stripes on his right arm, green barrack trousers and shiny black shoes. He'd need the warmth from these because soon he'd be outside, ready to prank the two young female nurses on night duty in Delhi Ward.

'Good and proper. I made sure I was sat next to them when they went to the dining room this evening Trevor. Curry night too, lovely scoff. I told them all about him, how he'd come a haunting, banging his drum really loud. They believed every word of it, even me telling them that tonight was the anniversary of his death, and that he'd come looking for someone to join him.'

'And they fell for it Malcolm?'

'Not half, I told them that anyone who heard it would die, they are going to shit themselves! They'll be listening out for his footsteps and beating drum.'

'It's just a shame you can't be there to see their faces Trevor. It'll just be our luck that the RSM will do a spot check and find us both out of the reception area.'

'When are you going to do it mate?'

'I thought just around midnight, the witching hour! I'll tie it in with doing the bed-state.'

They both sighed, they hated the nightly bed-state, having to go around each ward and asking for the numbers of patients, most of the nurses were too busy and they both hated the hanging around that went with it. Then they had to add them all up and get the correct tally to hand over to the Commanding Officer and Matron in the morning. Even the nurses had their own paperwork to do for the CO and Matron, their dreaded daily and nightly report. It had to be exactly written, in black ink, underlined red for the VSIL or SIL, the Very Seriously Ill Listed and Seriously Ill Listed. New admissions, deaths and unusual occurrences had to be written down neatly so that the heads of the hospital had a good idea of what was happening on their wards. For some nurses it was an added embuggerance, others used to have fun, like finding obscure words to use, so that the CO and Matron had to look out their dictionaries. Others would get together with other wards and try and sneak in song or film titles. These were then collected by the night sister or her colleague, the night extra, the senior was responsible for the smooth running of the building and staff during the long shift from 1930 hours through to about 0800 hours, whilst the night extra was a spare pair of hands, flitting from ward to ward, helping out where needed. If the night sister was friendly enough, then she would keep score and distribute the prize fund to the winning ward, but usually it was the night extra, the seasoned sergeant or warrant officer in on the jokes from when they were younger. After they'd taken a cut of course!

Malcolm and Trevor eyed up the oxygen cylinder spanner from the resuscitation trolley and the bin by their feet, little knowing that Scott and Naomi were silent watchers, waiting to see their prank unfold.

'Dorothy, I'm just going to check on Mrs Frances in bed twelve, her blood pressure was a bit low when I went around doing the TPRs and BPs at ten,' said the nurse in the grey dress and black shoes, she straightened her small paper hat as she stood up.

'Okay Victoria,' replied her colleague as she clicked her multi-coloured pen so that red ink was now selected. She'd wished that she had chosen to perform the nightly round of temperatures, pulses and respiratory rates along with blood pressures, rather than filling this form out, again. She was not noted for her tidy writing. She stretched and yawned, day four into a seven-night run, she was glad it was hump night, half way there. She'd enjoy her week off though, going back home to see her boyfriend. BANG! BANG! BANG! interrupted her thoughts. She sprinted from her desk to where the sound came from. She almost collided with Victoria, who had rushed back to her friend, believing safety in numbers.

'Do you think it's him,' quivered Victoria.

Another BANG! BANG! BANG! filled the tiny office space, as if answering her question.

'It's the 14th now, it has gone midnight, Malcolm was right.'

'No it can't be,' cried Victoria, 'there's no such thing as ghosts.'

As if disagreeing with her another BANG! BANG! BANG! resounded around the office.

Both nurses looked at each other, all eyes as large as saucers; they each glanced at the door, and ran out onto the ward, trying to get as far away as possible. 'It's the drummer boy, come to kill one of us,' they screamed in unison as they fled.

Trevor was squatted under the floorboards of the Delhi Hut ward, his back resting on one of the middle stilts. He'd scraped his knees getting into the small space, but thought a small injury so worth it. He'd placed himself under the office area, if things went wrong he didn't want to be on a charge for waking up the patients. But their prior planning and preparation had played off. Malcolm had played his role perfectly, he'd seen through the window how Dorothy had kept looking over her right shoulder every now and again whilst she wrote out her report, almost as if she expected a ghostie to appear in the doorway. He couldn't wait to get back to reception and share a laugh with Malcolm. He'd just give it a few minutes.

Scott and Naomi were in hysterics; they hadn't laughed together in such a long time. Tears of joy were running down Scott's cheeks, his stomach muscles were starting to hurt from the laughter. It was a welcome relief from the horrors of war. He forced himself to calm down because he wanted to ask Naomi something, he'd just give it a minute more, it brought him such joy to see such happy emotion on her face.

'So the hospital rumour mill thought that the drummer boy haunted their wards.'

'Yes,' replied Naomi collecting herself together. It's a bit like the name of Tidworth changing down the centuries. You know, like Chinese whispers.'

Scott nodded in agreement.

'The nurses and medical staff probably ran with the idea of the Tidworth demon drummer that Harold told you about at the Royal British Legion and with each new member of staff and generation of nurses and medics it probably got corrupted too, until they were left with the tale of a drummer boy who bangs his drums on the 14th February each year looking for someone about to die. Every military hospital and even civilian hospitals have their own ghost story; some even have several supposed ghosts. But wasn't that a cracker!'

'Aye, a pure belter!'

Naomi winked at him, a wicked grin spreading across her face, 'do you want to start another!'

'No, you aren't, are you...'

She did. She couldn't resist it. Trevor was still squatting down under the floorboards, he'd moved away from the stilt that was supporting his back and had crawled up towards the nurses as they ran the length of the ward, not caring if their patients were woken up. Fortunately, most were post-surgical and were still in a foggy haze of morphine and were sleepy from late afternoon anaesthetics. His shoulders were still shaking in mirth at the mischief he'd caused. In his left hand was the metal waste-paper bin, standard army green issue and with the crow's foot stamped on the bottom. The oxygen cylinder spanner was in his right hand. He was contemplating doing a few more bangs at this end of the ward now so that the two frightened nurses would think that they were being followed by the drummer boy. He hadn't realised that he, the hunter, had now become the prey.

Naomi blew onto her right hand, watching in fascination as it turned icy blue. She was crouched right behind Trevor, moving wraith-like into position. She waited until just before he was about to bang the spanner onto the bin. Then she silently lunged out her hand, clasped its frozen digits around his shoulder, where its icy steel cold penetrated deeply through his woollen jumper, searching out and finding his skin. She then whispered into his ear 'Have you seen my drum mister!'

Trevor gave out a high pitched scream, bumped his head on the floorboards and frantically crawled on all fours out of the gap below Delhi Hut. Once upright he sprinted through the awning-covered walkway as if Old Nick himself was after him. He left an unpleasant smell and a trail of dripping urine in his wake.

Chapter 32

'Oh, Naomi Scarlet, you are a bad, bad woman!' laughed Scott, still watching the receding RAMC corporal. He heard movement behind him, a noise also coming from under the stilts, under the ward. He turned around and had assumed it was a rat or a fox, grubbing about for an opportune meal on their nightly forage. But this was something much worse. Crawling on all fours towards him was the raggedy-haired woman. This time snakes were flowing from her mouth, slithering across to him, keeping abreast with her darting movements as they shuffled and slid towards him.

He startled visibly as Naomi said, 'don't worry haggis muncher, I'm right beside you. But this is your time now, you need to work this one out for yourself, but know that I am here.'

Scott quickly looked at Naomi, more for reassurance that she was definitely there, faith he thought, I can have faith in you, for sure. He turned back because the shuffling noises and the pitter patter of palms and feet on the leafy and dusty concrete had stopped. She was now right in front of him. Her heavy breathing suffocated him in this confined space. He was immobile, frozen once more as she cocked her head to the side, as if judging him. He could smell her rancid breath fill his nostrils with its fetid odour that clung to him like a clawing animated corpse trying to hang onto life. He gasped and involuntary coughed. A wicked grin crossed her mud streaked face as she now started to sniff around his face and neck.

'RUBIDUB DUM, RUBIDUB DUM, RUBIDUB DUM, RUBIDUB DUM,' sounded throughout the area, echoing and bouncing off the floorboards in this enclosed space. It was the real drummer boy making the noise, not the daft corporal playing tricks.

Scott could move now and he shuffled furiously backwards, almost in time to the beating drumsticks against the tightened skin of the drum that continued to resound, 'RUBIDUB DUM, RUBIDUB DUM, RUBIDUB DUM, RUBIDUB DUM.'

Naomi, as she promised, moved with him. They reached the last supportive stile and together pushed backwards on their hands and feet one final time, reaching the open air, much like a near drowned swimmer. Only Scott took no time for a life-saving breath of air as he emerged out from this fresh horror. He was straight onto his feet, ready to face her, to go one on one.

She did not disappoint, she was straight out, her hands and feet working in unison, furiously tapping on the floor, like a giant centipede running through a jungle floor. She then leapt out from beneath The Delhi hut and sprang onto Scott, wrapping her legs around his waist and grasping him close by the shoulders. She bit into his neck and Scott could feel warm liquid work its way down his left shoulder. He tried hopelessly to shake her off of him. Worms, spiders, beetles, cockroaches and all manner of insects teemed at his feet and swarmed up his legs, biting as they fought for space and the tasty prize of his skin and blood. He screamed out 'GET OFF ME!'

'Faith Scott; now is the time for your faith,' cried out Naomi.

'I have no faith, there is no God,' shrieked out Scott. 'I do not…'

'RUBIDUB DUM, RUBIDUB DUM, RUBIDUB DUM, RUBIDUB DUM, WHERE IS HE, RUBIDUB DUM, RUBIDUB DUM, RUBIDUB DUM, RUBIDUB DUM,' shouted out the woman, now staring straight into Scott's eyes, spittle flying into his mid-sentenced open mouth. The most cunning of the insects saw their chance and like a lava flow swept into his mouth.

Scott tried to spit them out and involuntary swallowed some, biting down on others, feeling their crunch, tasting their rankness. He leant forward as if to be sick, only she was still wrapped around him as if they were one flesh. They fell to the floor like two lovers collapsing onto a bed. Only this frenzy was survival, not love. And all the while she continued her mantra, 'RUBIDUB DUM, RUBIDUB DUM, RUBIDUB DUM, RUBIDUB DUM, WHERE IS HE, RUBIDUB DUM, RUBIDUB DUM, RUBIDUB DUM, RUBIDUB DUM.'

'THEN HAVE FAITH IN HER, SCOTT, YOUR MOTHER,' Naomi screamed to him.

Scott felt himself pound onto the floor, his fall broken by her, the woman who continued to scream out, 'RUBIDUB DUM, RUBIDUB DUM, RUBIDUB DUM, RUBIDUB DUM, WHERE IS HE, RUBIDUB DUM, RUBIDUB DUM,

RUBIDUB DUM, RUBIDUB DUM,' over and over again, her voice reaching operatic pitches in her fervour.

All around him vanished, the Delhi ward, built to look like a tropical hutted building had vanished. It suddenly went dark, like that instant darkness of the jungle, as the night life, the insects, took over. He felt himself engulfed, swarmed upon, entombed by them as they scuttled and clambered on and into him. He could feel himself suffocate, the slow death of the prolonged struggle for another breath that would not come as they swarmed down his throat and into his lungs, he could hear their pattering within him, he could hear 'THEN HAVE FAITH IN HER, SCOTT, YOUR MOTHER.'

'Yes,' he thought, 'my dying thoughts will be of my mother.'

He was a child again, at the end of the first day at school, and she was there waiting, as she had promised, at the school gate, waving merrily to him. He ran to her, wrapped his small arms around her legs, nuzzling into her stomach, as if trying to be reborn, breathing in her sweet motherly smells. Then realisation interrupted his memories and hit him like the shock of an unexpected slap across the face that stings but grabs your attention and causes sudden understanding to instantly dawn in your head like a bright-wakening summer sun. 'YOU ARE HIS MOTHER!' he screamed out. A flow of spent insects swarmed out of him, pushed further along like the darkest cloud before a rainstorm with each forced out, highly emotive word.

She was gone from under him. He took his chance and leapt up, despite his fatigue. Lights rose up, expelling the darkness, the evil all gone. As he turned he could see Naomi, smiling encouragingly at him, she was not alone.

There, beside Naomi, holding her hand; was the drummer boy. He looked about ten years old, his fair hair sticking out from his bearskin hat, his red tunic radiated against the brilliant whiteness of his cross belts. His drum was hanging by his kilted thigh, attached to his belts. His drumsticks were now hanging loose; he needed to drum no longer.

'Hello bonnie loon, that's a fair loud drum you have there,' smiled Scott, sensing, rightly, that his ordeal was finally over.

The drummer boy grinned back, and then looked over Scott's shoulder and his grin formed into the most beatific smile, 'MOTHER!' he shouted as he ran to Scott, dropping his drumsticks as he sprinted past and beyond him.

Scott turned around and watched, almost paternally, as the drummer boy ran into the welcoming, outstretched arms of his kneeling mother. There was no mud, blood or insects on her. Her shoulder length hair shone and gleamed in the sunshine that enveloped them as they finally embraced, two centuries apart forgotten in a blink of the eye. Her grey dress was clean and whole and swept down elegantly to her shoes, almost brushing them clean. She hung on tightly to her son, her brave little drummer boy. There was a blinding flash and then together, they vanished, two halves finally made whole.

Naomi put on a Scottish accent, 'Nae bad ma loon!'

'That was a rubbish accent quine. So is that it, she scares me witless, almost chokes me to death, and simply vanishes, not even a thank you?' said an incredulous Scott.

Naomi laughed, 'It's not all about you! But you did really well, you know yourself that there is a special bond between a mother and son, a bond that nothing can break, not even death. They are where they want to be, together.'

'And us?' asked Scott, hoping for the right answer.

'It's all about faith Scott, trust me!'

Author's Note

Thank you, dear reader, for your continuing support in my writing career. Scott's adventures will continue with a Christmas short story released late December and another novel in 2017. Although my itchy fingers are desperate to tap out a stand-alone novel with different characters and subjects and no amount of scratching will ease the itchiness. So why not follow me on www.facebook.com/cgbuswell and www.twitter.com/CGBUSWELL where I will post about its release.

I am most grateful to readers who have left reviews and feedback at Amazon and Good Reads for my first novel and short story. It would be wonderful if you could leave a review for The Drummer Boy at those sites or perhaps tell your friends about the books using the handy social media links at www.cgbuswell.com

Thanks

Chris

Acknowledgements

Isn't my daughter ever so talented! She has brought the drummer boy to life in her stunning artwork that adorns the front cover. Thank you Abigail, my cupcake! Angus would have been proud of your painting and your forthcoming graduation. Please don't put your fees up!

Good friends are so hard to find and I count myself lucky that 'Padre' Katherine and Ray Hyman of Cruden Bay IT Services www.crudenbaytraining.co.uk are such dear friends. Thank you for your support in this most difficult of years, Karla, Abigail and I are truly blessed to have you in our lives. Thank you for your eagle-eyed proofreading skills.

The lettering for the cover and my author website is from the talented Richard at www.rogue.co.uk who with a few words brief always produces such creative work. Thank you Richard.

Thank you Anne, the Aberdeenshire librarian, who seeks out so many reference books to help me with my 'faction' style of writing, you are wonderful. Please excuse the next subject matter!

The Army Medical Services Museum staff helped steer me in a new direction when we spoke about the drummer boy and spoke with such enthusiasm about Waterloo and provided several lightbulb moments. Thank you Ceri Gage, Jason Semmens and Gail Anderson; I'd dearly love to hold those teeth!

I'm grateful to Colin Clyne for the music and for allowing me to use his lyrics, hear Doin' Fine at www.colinclyne.com

Printed in Great Britain
by Amazon